AMY DORKSON

The Hollow Earth

Broomr

Contents

Chapter 1

It was a wet and stormy day, so much so that Andromedo and Kelly decided to hold off getting married maybe to the end of the day, or tomorrow, so they wouldn't make the courthouse floor slippery and therefore hazardous. Tabitha was having a very long and bad day, and it was about to get longer and worse. It started out with her and her handsome chunk of a husband Frankfurt getting so mad at each other that in the heat of the moment, they both regrettably agreed to taking a break from each other, something they both regretted as soon as they said it, but were both too proud and angry to admit to.

Furthermore, it turned out that amidst their adventuring and trying to be heroes, they had forgotten to pay their bills (for some reason, they thought her father-in-law, Gary, was going to do that for them, considering he was the one sending them on these quests), and so early that morning, they noticed an eviction notice on their door. Not even a gosh-damn courtesy knock or anything. Just something to discover first thing in the morning. This cemented Tabitha's opinion that her landlord was afraid of her, on account of her being a witch that he was evicting. She was so mad her kids had to talk her out of cursing the man, because they all knew that she was particularly good at cursing people and that she'd regret it later.

Her landlord was a Rurulian man named Kingsley with a full head of white hair and bright pink skin and would put you in the mind of an angry boss at a newspaper, and he was indeed terrified of Tabitha. It didn't help that they were neighbors. It all started one day when she was walking with her kids and fussing at them for fighting. Kingsley, a misophonic man, stuck his head outside his door and said, "Gosh-damnit, shut the hell up!" Tabitha paused for effect. She turned around, and a tumbleweed rolled past her, and Western music played in the background as a magical effect of her mood at being talked to this way. She smiled at the man. "Excuse me, sir, I didn't hear you, what did you say?" Her teeth glinted in the sunlight. At that moment, he knew, this woman was scary. "I'm sorry, uh, please keep it down." She kept smiling, albeit now hiding her teeth. "Yes, sir, will do." And walked off with her children.

So, when it came time to put an eviction notice on her door, especially hearing about how she was a witch (he had a long-standing phobia of witches, ever since the mean old lady down the street put a curse on him for sticking his tongue out at her), he was careful 1) not be there when she saw it and 2) put the extra words on there Sorry, Please Don't Curse Me. As well as, If You Can Pay Me Back Soon, We'll Call It Even. It was, indeed, the politest eviction notice Tabitha had ever gotten, and also the only one because she made gosh-damn sure to pay her bills on time.

She called up her father-in-law, Gary. It rang a few times and he answered.

"Hello?"

"Hi Dad," she called him Dad at his request, "Did you remember to pay our bills while we were gone with the money we gave you?"

"Pfft, I was going to pay with my own money and give you all your money back," said Gary. Tabitha patiently waited for him to understand the implications of what he just said. "Oh, hell, I forgot. I'm so sorry, Tabitha."

"It's okay, Gary, but could you get that money to my landlord so he doesn't evict us?" she asked patiently. It paid to be patient with your in-laws. If nothing else, not being the hated out-law made patience with in-laws totally worthwhile. Gary and Tabitha had a great relationship. Despite that Gary was a notorious gangster, to Tabitha, he would always be the sweet doddering old man she'd met when she was a teenager, who treated her as if she was his own daughter.

"Absolutely," said Gary, putting Tabitha at ease right before metaphorically pulling the rug out from underneath her, "I just have to find it first... I'm so sorry."

Tabitha took a deep breath and tried to stabilize herself. "It's okay, Dad. If I work really hard, I think I can make back the money between then and now."

"I really am very sorry."

"No, it's fine, totally." Gary kept apologizing so Tabitha made an excuse to leave the conversation. "Don't worry, Dad, just find the money when you can and until then, I've been really wanting to throw myself into work, anyway. I love you. Goodbye." And she hung up before Gary could do any more apologizing.

Chapter 2

Tabitha took a deep breath and tried to center herself. It wasn't every day that your best friends were getting married, husband left you, and you got an eviction notice. She looked through her window at the outside where it was raining heavily and decided that it was lucky it was raining, because that meant that Kelly and Andromedo were putting off their wedding until later on that evening, which meant that she had more time to make money between then and now to pay off her landlord. Because who knew how long it would take Gary, who was not only a notorious gangster but also notoriously messy, to find the money she'd given him? Old age was making him forgetful.

It was also lucky to be raining because broomstick ride sharers (did I mention that she had a ride sharing service on her broomstick?) made more money on particularly rainy days. People were willing to pay more to get from point A to point B on days where the sky was pouring down on them, and they dug Tabitha's dryness charm, something not all of these witches were able to master.

Tabitha had her own problems when it came to witchery. 1) She was too good at cursing, and a woman could end up in prison that way. (Not that she had but she could.) 2) She was absolute crap at herbs and stuff and probably could accidentally kill a person if she didn't already have that reputation. 3) She only had warts on her toes, which didn't make her look bona fide at all as a witch. A proper witch should have a wart on her nose, at least. This was actually a matter of vanity; every time a wart tried to surface on her face, she magicked it away, and only kept the warts on her toes so she wouldn't get kicked out of her coven. (Precious little has been written about Tabitha's coven, partially because they operate in secret and partially because the author forgot amidst writing about Tabitha's other adventures.)

Chapter 3

Her first customer was a chimera who was part baboon and part human. She didn't ask him his name but he looked familiar. She was proud of her world view which was very tolerant of both humans and chimeras, and looked at it as a positive her customer was part-baboon, because that meant that he was easier to lift on account of not being as heavy as a regular human. He was wearing a blue velvet suit that had just a bit of wear and tear on it, and had beautiful auburn hair covering his whole body (that she could see, though, as we all know, that doesn't include a baboon's butt, for some reason).

To be culturally sensitive, she didn't ask him if he'd heard the president of Irrorria's rap song, My Majestic Baboon Butt, because baboon chimeras didn't like that question and she wasn't about to go getting a reputation as a culturally insensitive ride sharer. She also didn't tell him that he looked like the president of Irrorria, even though he most certainly did look just like him, because she didn't want people to think that she couldn't tell one baboon chimera from the next.

Instead, to be polite and hopefully get better tips, she asked him about himself.

"I hope you're having a great day today," she told him, which was her way of asking him how his day was, but trying to steer him in the direction of having a good one.

"It has most certainly not been a good day," said the guy, pompously. He sniffed, and, despite the heavy rain around them that had already drenched her customer prior to his stepping into her dry zone of a broomstick (remembering she does some pretty swell dryness charms), she suspected that he might be crying.

"What's wrong, if you don't mind me asking?" she asked, hoping he wouldn't get mad at her. She could definitely feel him crying now. A few drops hit her on the back and soaked through her black work witch's dress. He shuddered a little bit.

"My butler turned on me!"

Tabitha didn't know how to respond to this. She, despite being a deposed queen (she was deposed as a toddler and had been in hiding ever since then, making her, despite her beginnings, very blue collar), had no memory of ever having had a butler. What did it even mean for a butler to turn on a person? Was he maliciously gossiping about him to the other servants? And how could you even ask a question like that without being rude?

"I am so sorry to hear that," said Tabitha. "What happened?"

The guy broke down into even more tears, making poor Tabitha supremely uncomfortable, as she didn't know how to deal with emotions like that. He wiped his tears with his arm.

"It's too soon to talk about it," he said.

Now what had happened, is something that we can know even if Tabitha does not know about it, because we just can. That's how it works. What had happened was that Tabitha was indeed giving a ride to the president of Irrorria, President George Franklington, and he was crying heavily because he'd been betrayed by his butler and long-time-best-friend Edington.

But what he didn't know was that this was not Edington's fault. Despite the two of them often joking that Edington hadn't assassinated him, yet, neither of them ever expected for Edington to actually assassinate George. It was a joke. But now poor George was having to take it seriously, because Edington really was trying to assassinate him.

It all started back in Irrorria, deep in the jungle, inside the Tree of Knowledge, which also served as a little town, a bed and breakfast, a convention center, and a bar. For context, it was one of those ridiculously big red cedar trees, and Edington was in the convention center with a know-it-all baboon chimera named Bonny, who was also very pretty (even though Edington was really holding his heart out for a human computer scientist named Rigoria Kingsmith), and a bunch of other anti-political baboon chimeras of all walks of life who were holding signs like, "Down with Politics!" and "Throw Poop At Politicians!" Edington hadn't expected this at all, and would have only gone to such an event to quickly disappear from it and warn his friend the president. (Despite his lifelong salty nature, he was actually quite loyal to the president, which would make his future betrayal hurt all the more deeply.)

He had just finished asking if this was a stationary get-together, when he was informed that, no, indeed, they were on the move, and this was just their meeting place. It was then that Bonny smiled at him, showing him all of her baboon teeth, and stuck him in the neck with a needle attached to a syringe full of mind-control drugs.

"That'll do it," Bonny said, gently unsticking the needle from Edington's neck. Edington would have panicked, but something in the drugs she just gave him prevented him from doing that. "How are you feeling, Edington, old boy?"

Edington thought about it. "This isn't the worst feeling in the world, but in the logic center of my brain, I feel betrayed. I've done nothing to you, and yet you've stuck me in the neck with a needle. Please tell me that's a cooties vaccine!" Under his breath, "I've already had a cooties vaccine, but I suppose another one won't hurt."

Cooties on their world was a horrific disease that made your face fall off, but there were controversial vaccinations for it.

"Oh-ho-no-no," said Bonny. "What I've given you makes you more susceptible to suggestions."

"I'm more susceptible to suggestions."

"You're going to do whatever I say."

Edington tried to fight what was happening inside of him, but despite all of his better efforts not to say it, he said, "I'm going to do whatever you say."

The crowd had gone quiet, listening to what Bonny was doing to poor Edington. They were very excited to see it, like vultures around recent roadkill.

"I want you to assassinate President George Franklington," she said, eyes lighting up with insane purpose. Edington's heart wrenched and he tried to figure out a way around this.

"You want me to assassinate President George Franklington," repeated George, actively listening but rather wishing that he wasn't. "Why? What did George ever do to you?"

"You know," said Bonny, looking very debonair, "it isn't him so much as what he represents. He's a puppet, and killing him gets us closer to the puppet master, and then we can take over the country and run it the correct way."

"And what way is that?" asked Edington, desperately trying to hold onto the last remnants of control of his mind.

"With peace and equality and brotherhood for all except for

our enemies, which we will brutally slaughter," said Bonny, uncharacteristically honest.

"I don't want to be a part of that," said Edington pathetically. The other baboons laughed at him, shrilly.

"That doesn't matter," said Bonny coldly. "You will murder the president of Irrorria, George Franklington."

The "medicine" coursing through Edington's veins, was fully operational now.

"I will murder the president of Irrorria, George Franklington."

Chapter 4

Despite his earlier reticence to speak, George Frankling-ton relayed what he knew about the story to Tabitha, basically that Edington tried to assassinate him.

"Wow, your butler tried to assassinate you?" repeated Tabitha, shocked.

"Yes, so I need you to fly me around for a while, and keep an eye out for malicious baboons on brooms, in case he knows where I'm at," said George. Somewhere in the more mercenary part of Tabitha's brain, coins ca-chinged, thinking that she would definitely be making good money today.

"Question."

"Mm-hmm."

"Why would your butler try to assassinate you? Are you a famous person? Or perhaps do the two of you have personal beef?"

"No, we've always solved on personal beef the way baboons do, by throwing poop at each other. Though I suppose you could call me famous."

Tabitha said, "I am literally dying right now to know who you are."

George got a small smile from her hyperbole. "I am the president of Irrorria, George Franklington."

Tabitha was so shocked to have such a celebrity on board that she almost dropped him, though she quickly corrected course, as not to make an ass out of herself in front of a famous person (again).

"What? I thought you looked like him!"

"I bet you thought you were being culturally sensitive not to ask me about it," said George wryly.

"I did think that! Oh, boy, was I foolish!"

"Nah, don't worry about that," said George, feeling as though he wanted his chauffeur to think he was cool. And she did think he was cool. He had a literal rap song commissioned about his butt and was so bold as to dance in buttless pants *himself* for the music video. Not that Tabitha considered those things to be truly cool; she considered that he was being nice to her, despite being a famous dude and her being decidedly not-famous, to be cool. "I'm glad for the help. And the company."

It was at this point that Tabitha remembered that she and Frankfurt were taking a break, something she deeply regretted. (And though she didn't know it, Frankfurt deeply regretted it too.) She worked to keep her back stiff and unemotional as a few tears dropped from her eyes. Though she sometimes considered divorcing Frankfurt, for not taking good care of his health, or for thinking she was crazy when she was probably less crazy than the average person, she didn't want to actually divorce him. She loved him so much it was painful.

It was a long story as to why they were on a break. Tabitha had kissed the wrong guy a few times over the course of their years together, in order to put a sleeping spell on him, because he was an agent of the state that could have her life ended for being a deposed queen. (Being a royal was deeply illegal in their world. So was math, up until very recently, upon which the countries of Irrorria and Gargantua had bravely decriminalized it.) Anyway, the agent of the state was also a police officer, was being the operative word, because he was fired after alleged ugly rumors about him, so he and his brother got jobs as exotic dancers, which was unfortunate because Tabitha had bought the services of exotic dancers (not knowing who would show up) for her friend Kelly's bachelorette party. Frankfurt showed up and saw this other man who'd Tabitha had kissed for her life and freedom, along with his lookalike brother (they were twins), and got really angry.

So the two of them argued throughout the night and into the morning, where, completely exhausted and still really angry with each other, they angrily called it quits and Frankfurt packed himself a small bag and left to go stay at Andromedo's house. (I'll tell you how that's going, later, but, long story short, Andromedo and Kelly did not want to be jinxed by Tabitha and Frankfurt's marital problems, especially considering that they were just about to get married.)

"Are you okay, ma'am?" asked George, noticing that his chauffeur hadn't spoken for a while even though he's spoken to her. As a fellow who'd been married for a long time and had multiple affairs with hypergamous women, he was attuned to the feelings of women around him. Because he had so much experience with women, especially at his age.

"I'm okay, it's just..." She would have continued with some excuse having nothing to do with the sorry state of her marriage currently (because she had some very old-fashioned ideas about professionalism and keeping her private life away from her work life, not that she did so great at that with Sergeant Marybeth, the traitor, long story still), when suddenly George yelled "Duck!" and instinctively, Tabitha ducked the broomstick just before some poop with a knife in it swept by them. "Holy crap!"

Her friend Harley was the one on the other broom, and she had a look on her face that was entirely unlike her normal cheerful expression, as if she'd been put under mind-control and now had no agency of her own. Behind Harley was a suited baboon, a chimera, wearing a similar expression.

"This is how you all try to kill each other?" asked Tabitha. "I don't know whether to be more grossed out or impressed by how well that would work. So, if the cut doesn't kill you, the sepsis does. It is kind of genius."

The ride was beginning to have more of a feel of an amusement park ride, as they did loop-de-loops through the air, trying to avoid the flying stink-bombs. "Normally our kind fights to the death when we try to kill each other," he said, struggling to talk around all of the totally unnecessary excitement, "but as of yet, neither Edington nor I have ever tried to kill anybody."

Harley kept trying to use her broom to knock George off of Tabitha's broom, hitting Tabitha in the process. Tabitha felt really some kind of way about this; she'd literally invited Harley to a bachelorette party that took place yesterday, and this was how she was treating her!

Tabitha knew Harley well enough to know that she had to be under some kind of spell, or something, because she literally never acted like this, and Tabitha had never wronged her so much as to deserve such treatment. Harley was a sweetheart. Tabitha could have thrown a bachelorette party with no strippers, and Harley would have just been happy to be invited.

"They have to be under some kind of bad magic," said Tabitha, "because Harley isn't acting like herself at all."

"Do you know of any magic that can do this to a person?"

asked George, hope in his voice.

"No, not unless it was drug induced. You know how it is. If we can't understand it, we call it magic."

"So you think they've been drugged?"

"Absolutely 150%."

"How do you know?"

"Harley has no beef with me, and I'm too unimportant to assassinate."

"What if she was bought out?"

"I didn't even stop to consider that, but I think she would look like either determined or apologetic in the face, if she was bought out."

Tabitha did some very complicated flying to lose her friend and the would-be-assassin. It took about thirty minutes, but soon they were flying in a crowded city, through sky scrapers where it was easier to hide.

"Question."

"Shoot."

"Weren't you in Irrorria, like, yesterday?"

"I was."

"How did you get here so fast? Especially from the jungle?"

"My secret service stays around me with a private jet," said George pompously.

"Yeah, but why not stay with the private jet?"

"It was exploded."

"Woah! Did that make the news already?"

"No, I try to keep things that make me look weak out of the news."

"Hm, sounds about right."

"What do you mean by that?"

"Well, what person in political power wants to look weak,

right? I'm sure political cartoons of you flying on the back of a fat witch's broomstick wouldn't do your political career any favors."

"Might help me amongst heavier women, and witches. Times have changed. Men can ask for help from women. That's not a weakness. Getting a plane blown up is a weakness. Especially when it's your right hand man who did it."

Tabitha thought it would be in her better interests as a business woman not to mention that he had been crying. Shit, she would be crying, too, if her right-hand man was trying to kill her. Her right-hand man was Frankfurt. She might cry just thinking about how they were recently broken up.

A fan of the series heard about this and went, "Noooo!" And I had to give the fan some spoilers to cheer her up. I won't do that to you. For all you know, the power couple of blue collar lazybodies are on a break. Because we all know readers don't want spoilers, even when you're deeply disappointing them.

"So what's going wrong in your life?" asked George, flirting because it was in his nature to flirt prolifically.

"ARBOR, nothing you need to know about, no offense, Mr. President."

Chapter 5

ARBOR was the name of their god, a quite obese fellow that was a salesman of stuff magicked out if the air. People thought of him as ARBOR, but not The ARBOR. He was just some dude. The ARBOR allegedly wanted human sacrifice, and people were serious about it. This ARBOR disapproved of human sacrifice and wished that people would stop doing that in his name. A lot of stuff needed to be cleared up. He could also shape-shift. Funny Tabitha saw an obese dude. He did that on purpose, he knew that would make him more relatable to her.

ARBOR was a guy who sold things to Tabitha and whose name just so happened to be used when people wanted a handy wordy dird. He sold meat, primarily, also vegetables. It was magicked from nothing, because allegedly he had that power. (He really had it, it wasn't just alleged.) This he thought might solve the Vegan Phenomenon that had swept through the planet ever since The Great Chimera Experiment, which created a whole knew kind of sometimes humanoid being that looked like your food sometimes which made it weird. Anyway, eventually people just wanted to be vegan whether or not the meat was ethically magicked out of the air. Which totally killed ARBBOR's business, except for Tabitha who felt sorry for him so therefore sometimes bought meat for her father-in-law, who was old-school and knew ARBOR personally and trusted him to have magicked from nothing meat.

"So what are you suggesting here?" asked George.

"That I drop you off and move onto my next customers so that I don't leave everybody hanging for the day. I doubt you have enough money to continue my services more than my other customers. I hope the best for you. May your friend overcome their bad magic and not kill you, same as my friend with me."

"I'm the president my money is no issue here, keep flying!"

"Yes, sir, no issue." A beat, to make conversation. "So you and the missus have been married for a long time, right? I've been married to my guy for most of my life, and he's a sweetheart, but currently he's angry at me and I'm angry at him, but normally we do quite well. What do you do to keep your marriage longevitous?"

"Well..." George thought about this. "I have no idea why my wife has put up with me as long as she has. I think perhaps having very low standards for a spouse might have something to do with it."

"Oh, my husband is the best of the best," said Tabitha, "which makes it all the worse that he is angry with me. I wish he wouldn't be. Though I could judo chop him right now to make a point."

"I've got quite a great wife," said the president suddenly. "Did I tell you, you could call me George? You can call me George."

"Hi George."

"What's your name again?"

"My name is Tabitha. There's not much interesting about me.

I'm a wife of near twenty years now and I have five amazing kids, and I don't want to make you dislike me by bragging too much about my good fortune."

"It's good to run into people who care about family," said George presidentially.

Tabitha got a dinging noise on her cell phone, checked and said, "My best friend is in need of a ride to her wedding. Do you want to go to a wedding? While you're waiting on your indeed under the influence of a spell or something friend to overcome their malaise, I can be your bodyguard."

The president laughed and laughed. Tabitha patiently waited on him to quit laughing.

"I'm serious, I actually have a background in self-defense," she said. "Hire me as security and I won't let you down."

"What's a background in self-defense mean?"

"Means I'm the meanest motherrespector out there who is also a witch and I went through years of fight club training. I am a master of self-defense. So, defending you should be no issue. I will not let your butler kill you."

"Okay. Did I notice that you're flying to your friend's house, now? I sensed a purposeful change in directions."

"Yes. It is time to pick them up to take them their wedding."

"Oh, okay, well, on with it, then."

Tabitha flew as quickly as she could to Kelly and Andromedo's apartment. A lot was going on there at the time. Her home looked as if there was a party going on.

"Tabitha, thank ARBOR you're here. I'm getting married today!" This was Kelly. She was dressed in the most beautiful wedding dress Tabitha had ever seen on anybody, looking as beautiful as a rainbow ending in sunshine buttercups, herself, flushed kind of purple, her eyes bright, really looking as gorgeous as anyone ever had in such a beautiful dress. She was jumping up and down and in general being very girly as she was getting married that day. She was vibrating with positive energy, and some chaotic neutral energy as well. Every once in a while, she'd yell at someone, but not in such a way to really hurt anybody's feelings.

"I thought you guys were eloping, but it seems as though everybody's showed up for it," said Tabitha, full of happy feeling because her best friends were getting married. She also felt guilty, like a traitor, for having dated Andromedo all those years ago. Tabitha was a little bit bipolar, so she ended up often feeling guilty unnecessarily. They were teenagers then and she had no idea that her best friend would one day be marrying the guy, otherwise, she'd have never dated him. Now they were all in their thirties. What a strange time to be feeling guilty. Maybe it was because she could never admit to having dated him. For some stupid reason, Tabitha kept lying every time confronted with the question, "Did you date Andromedo when you were teenagers?" And would say, "No," and pretend to only be into dudes with dolphin fins, like her husband.

Did I mention that Frankfurt was part chimera and therefore had a dolphin tail fin on his tail bone? He was a big, burly fellow, with the build of a football player turned dad, and his tail fin was the bane of his existence, because people loved to pick on him about his tail fin. As if that wasn't specist. He and Kelly were also cousins.

Kelly finally noticed President George Franklington. "Tabitha, why is the president of Irrorria at my home?" None of her friends actually liked the guy, because they didn't like his buffoonery, like throwing poop when he gets angry, or letting a math camp exist in his country (math camps were where mathematicians went when math was illegal, terrible places to be, a place were mathematicians died regularly). Anyway, they didn't know that he was behind the funding for the explosions at the math camp that freed so many mathematicians. Considering how long it took for him to get to that, they'd probably still dislike him upon knowing that, but less than they would have otherwise, slightly.

"My ride-sharing service just turned into a security service as well. I am in charge of hiding George Franklington for reasons that are kind of a long story, though I'd be happy to tell you about it at more opportune timing. Basically, I'm being paid to prevent an assassination attempt."

"I can think of no better reason for you to bring the President George Franklington to my wedding," said Kelly definitively. "And I'll give him a chance, who knows, he might have redeem-ing qualities."

"He is nice to service workers," Tabitha said.

"Oh that's nice, I like him better already," said Kelly. "A tiny bit. It's as if a dictator was found to be personable to the poors."

President George Franklington was smiling and nodding as if he was playing cards and this was his particular poker face. "I appreciate honest feedback." He twitched a little the tiniest bit, in his eye. "But you don't know the whole story."

"I know you kept people in math camps who were starving and getting killed and used for slave labor," Kelly snapped.

"Right, I never understood what the problem with math was. So I arranged to get them escaped."

"Your command of Gargantuan is abominable."

"I'm sure your Irrorrian isn't so great, either."

"So how did you get them escaped, so to say?" asked Kelly.

"I paid a man to set up strategic bombings. The Great Bombing of the Math Camp was funded by me."

"Well, that's cool," said Kelly. "Sort of, you could have just officially shut it down."

"I tried but it wasn't going fast enough for me so I paid for the bombings."

"Okay, I officially hate you less than I used to," said Kelly. She smiled at the president and said, "Welcome to my wedding day!" And made more girly-dolphiny noises of happiness, still vibrating with positivity. Then she remembered to explain to Tabitha, "My parents are paying for us to have a church wedding. They just sprang it out of nowhere and invited everybody at last minute who all jumped to come to the wedding. It'll still happen later on today."

"Wow, when did this happen?"

"I found out about it just a few minutes ago, right after talking to you."

"Do you still need me here right now?"

"I will later. Sorry, I should have called you, I'm just over-whelmed at the moment."

"No, it's totally fine."

"I'm about to kick everybody out of my house for a little bit so I can get ready."

"That's cool, I'll see you in a little bit. Might still have this guy with me. Probably will." And then in an undertone, just so Kelly could hear her. "If that's okay."

"It's okay, I'm going to make him perform the rap song for my wedding," said Kelly, very seriously.

Just after Tabitha left Kelly's house with George, that's when Frankfurt arrived at Kelly's house. He was wearing a suit.

"Wedding's not until later," Kelly told Frankfurt. "Though I admire that you're already ready for it. You're a good best man."

"Thank you," Frankfurt told Kelly.

"Did you arrive here on a broomstick?"

"I might have."

"I thought only women were allowed to fly those." A beat. "Is that a wig peaking out of your satchel?" Frankfurt blushed. "Is that a pocketbook?"

"What is this, 20 questions?" asked Frankfurt. "Where's Andromedo?"

"He's getting ready in our room. Neither of us have seen each other since this morning, for good luck."

"I've never understood wedding superstitions," said Frankfurt. Kelly gave him an evil eye. "But I respect them... I'm going to go say hi to Andromedo."

"You do that," Kelly said, annoyed with her cousin for no particular reason. Maybe it was because Andromedo loved him so much.

Frankfurt walked back into Andromedo's room, finding Andromedo dressed in a suit and seated in front of the TV, a controller in his hands, playing a videogame. It took Frankfurt a moment to realize that Andromedo was playing The Great Chimera Experiment, which was a historical game.

"Bro, you got local multiplayer?" Frankfurt asked. Andromedo looked up and smiled, realizing his buddy was there.

"I do, grab a controller!"

Chapter 6

"Can we visit my mother?" asked George. "It's so rare that I'm in Gargantua to be able to visit her. Also, I should tell her that I'll probably be dead soon."

"Sure, and don't insult my security abilities," said Tabitha. "I might look like an overweight mother, because I am one, but nobody's going to assassinate you on my watch!"

"I suppose you'll want extra compensation."

"I charge 8 rupees an hour for security, and 3 rupees per mile flown."

"That's reasonable, I was expecting more."

"What were you expecting?"

"9 rupees per hour for security and 4 rupees per mile flown."

"Can I charge you that?"

"Sure, you're the bodyguard. Is it wrong if I look forward to possibly seeing you engaged in hand-to-hand combat? It's not weird, I just can't imagine it but it sounds spectacular."

"You wouldn't be the first to say that to me," said Tabitha. Tabitha, being a blue collar deposed royal, spent her childhood being occasionally abducted by the local rang (royal gang) The Lionhearted, to get her in a fight club they put all their child relatives through to keep them tough and able to defend themselves. Something that she knew but not most people knew, was that you could tell who was in a rang by the fact that they called each other rang. Like, "What's up, rang? How are you doing?" It was like a secret code; they weren't allowed to tell outsiders about this.

"I admire your friend, Kelly," said George. "Often when you're a high ranking politician, like me, people act sycophantically and won't give their true opinions, but that is not so with your friend Kelly."

"That's true, Kelly's a sweet lady but she is no sycophant."

"When you work in politics, honesty is social capital. Perhaps she should be in politics."

"I'd vote for her. Though I don't know how viable that would be for her; I think she's too honest for politics."

"Maybe; that's a thing. I need you to turn left at that fork."

"Will do. I'm supposing your mother's house is nearby?"

"Yes, it's the 8th house on the left."

George Franklington's mother's house was surprisingly small, perhaps a 1 bedroom house, and his mother was a human woman in her 80s who was missing teeth and it seemed some of her memory. Her name was Aida Franklington.

"Why hello there," she said. Tabitha could make out some similarities in features between George and Aida, but Aida's lines were deeper and she was a full human. She was wearing a white pajama gown and a pink robe with pink bedroom slippers, and she had some rollers in her hair that looked as if they were put in a week ago and forgotten about. "Come on inside, it's so rare that I get visitors."

George and Tabitha followed Aida into the house, which smelled like vegetable stew, like she cohabitated with cats, and read lots of newspapers. This was true: Aida was a newspaper hoarder. The whole floor was covered in newspapers, and some newspapers covered cat droppings and other newspapers. There were an indeterminate number of cats inside.

"It's lovely here," said Tabitha politely. "How many cats do you have?"

"Hmm? Oh, I don't know, it seems that number changes twice a day. And you are?"

"Tabitha Walker, your son's bodyguard and chauffeur."

"Who's my son?"

"Here I am, Mother," said President George Franklington, looking at that moment his most humble and good looking. As if he was attempting to turn the charm on his mother.

"Oh, there you are! It's good to see you again, my good boy!" She leaned a little bit to hug her son, who was shorter than her. "I almost forgot that I had a son. It's been terribly long since you've visited me last."

"I'm sorry, Mother," said George, keeping an arm around his mother. "I'm the president of Irrorria now so I don't get much time off to visit family."

"Oh, well, you should change that," scolded Aida, pointing with a gnarled finger. "You're the president so you make the rules."

"Not entirely," said George with a good-natured laugh. "I still have rules that predate me that I have to follow."

"Oh rules, smools," Aida teased. "Would you all like some vegetable stew?"

Tabitha's stomach rumbled fiercely. "Oh, that would be lovely, I haven't had anything to eat all day."

"I would love some of your vegetable stew, Mother," said George.

"Psst," said Tabitha to George, "why do you call your mom Mother instead of Mom or any of the other maternal variations?"

"This is how rich people talk."

"But your mother here is not rich."

"Don't let her fool you, she just likes to live humbly."

"Oh, cool, yeah I always thought big houses meant more cleaning. If I lived alone, I'd only have the need for the one bedroom."

"I don't like big houses and fancy things," said Aida, loudly, "and I don't like other people cleaning up after me."

Tabitha was not judgmental in this respect and had noted nonjudgmentally that Aida didn't like picking up after herself, either. Either that or she just forgot a good chunk of the time. Aida ladled out their stew for them, and each took a bowl.

"Mmm," said Tabitha, and not to be outdone, "Mmm!" said George, "Tastes just like it did when I was growing up." George said, after a few bites, "Mother, I have something to tell you."

Aida put an arm over George's shoulder. "What is it my boy?" A beat. "I mean my young man."

"Oh, it's been a long time since anybody's called me young, thank you for that," said George, "and I have to tell you, you might be outliving me."

"No!" said Aida, even louder than usual. (Aida was a little bit deaf, that's why she talked so loudly.) "Don't tell me you've got cancer or something terminal like that. Unless you do. You don't do you?"

"No, Mother, worse. I'm going to get assassinated."

"He is not going to be assassinated," interjected Tabitha, loudly. "I keep telling him that I will protect him from assassination. I'm his body guard."

"Oh, wow, young lady, I had no idea you had such a skill set."

"I'm definitely skilled enough to keep your son alive and have helped him escape totally free from a previous assassination attempt earlier today."

"So somebody is trying to assassinate my son today?"

"Yes. But I stopped him."

"How did you do that?"

"I fly a broomstick normally for a living, doing ride sharing, and was able to maneuver in such a way that they were not able to catch up with us or do George here any damage."

"Oh, so you're a witch?"

"Yes, ma'am."

"That's cool. I always regretted not going into witchery. Several members of my family are all witches and it's been working out fantastically for them. I see nowadays they're more progressive and don't absolutely require you to have a wart on your nose."

"Yeah, somehow I managed to escape having a wart on my nose," said Tabitha. She used to have a wart on her nose but Frankfurt complained about it so she put some ointment on it and it went away. It was the store-bought kind of ointment, no magic involved.

"So how did you get into body-guarding?" asked Aida.

"Well, I saw the opportunity today after your son's first assassination attempt of the day..."

"That you know about," interjected George.

"That I know about, and so I posited to him that I would make a great body guard on account of my extensive knowledge of the self-defense-arts and science."

"Which you learned in?" asked Aida.

"Fight club, ma'am." There were no rules to fight club, other than no snitching. That was The Lionhearted rang's rules. But they were allowed to use fight club affiliation to get jobs.

"Oh, I read about that in the newspaper. So you've been able to fight good almost your entire life then?"

"Yes, ma'am."

"That's good, I need a strong woman to protect my little ickle Georgie." It seemed for a moment she forgot that Georgie was a grown president, not a baby. George tolerated this. "Not like his harridan of a wife."

"Mother!"

"I'm sorry, you know I always tell the truth."

Tabitha liked Aida but felt very sorry for George Frankling-ton's wife. Must be rough for the poor woman, being disliked by her mother-in-law. Tabitha didn't have a mother-in-law to dislike her, because her mother-in-law died of breast cancer, and she did remember her from forever ago when she was alive. Frankfurt's mother was really nice, for the most part.

"We should also visit my wife, now that you remind me."

"Isn't she in Irrorria?" asked Tabitha.

"No, she's in Gargantua, too. Visiting family."

"I had no idea that there were so many Irrorrians in Gargan-tua," said Tabitha with perhaps insensitive honesty.

"Oh, yeah, there are also a lot of Gargantuans in Irrorria."

"Mathematicians."

"Not just mathematicians, and I just decriminalized it, so can I get a break about it?"

"I think that's part of the problem, giving people breaks about it when they're responsible for people dying..."

"I literally emancipated them."

"So you say." Then, "Doesn't matter, I'm here to get you to point A and then to point B and now points C and D, and to keep you from getting assassinated."

Tabitha was beginning to rethink her hypothesis that the butler was on drugs. What if he was paid off? Or maybe he just held a serious grudge over something or another. George was thinking the same thing. Then again, Harley also had that look on her face, which made Tabitha further expect that maybe they were on drugs. Tabitha blamed a lot on drugs and alcohol, habitually, to keep her kids from doing drugs and alcohol.

"Bye, Miss Aida, it was nice meeting you," said Tabitha to Aida, giving her a hug because her vegetable stew was delicious.

"Oh, thank you, it was nice meeting you too."

"Good-bye, Mother, I do hope to see you again one day," said George solemnly.

"Good-bye, my dear, do stay safe."

"I will try my best." And off they went.

Chapter 7

"So where is Mrs. Franklington staying?" asked Tabitha.

"She's at the Rich Harlot hotel."

"Oh, I know the place. We learned about its original proprietress in school. She's a historical figure."

"Right, a rich harlot, she had a great imagination but not necessarily in naming, she just named it after herself kind of," said George. "But it's one of the fanciest hotels in Gargantua."

"I am very excited to be going there. I never thought of this as a place where I could do ride sharing, but I bet the ride sharers around there make bank."

"Most of us take limousines."

"Oh, why's that?"

"Fancier than using a witch ride share."

"I would always rather fly through the open air than ride in a limousine."

Tabitha had gone through many illustrious jobs and careers in the path to finding her professional self, and really who she was professionally, her true self, was being a broomstick ride sharer. They said that if you did what you liked as a job, it wouldn't feel like you were working, and that's kind of how it felt for Tabitha on a good day. (On a bad day, it was definitely work.)

Other jobs she had done included dish washing (her family

was full of dishwashers), security, stewardess, house cleaner, etc. etc. etc. The nice thing about flying on a broomstick was that she was impervious to the weather, for the most part (it still wasn't smart to go out in the middle of a thunderstorm or tornado, no matter how magical a woman was).

The weather was drying up a little bit, at least it wasn't torrentially downpouring and Tabitha's force-field around the broomstick and riders had the neat effect of the light raindrops beading off of it and rolling down, past the force-field and eventually to the ground.

Tabitha was flying into the wealthier part of the country, into the big city to a skyscraper with the name in lights both at ground level and in the sky: The Rich Harlot.

"Follow me," said George. "Normally I wouldn't ask, but I need to be not assassinated."

"No, definitely, I'll do my best to keep you assassination-free," said Tabitha, very serious about it. She followed him into the hotel. "Just to be clear, your wife is absolutely here, right? Because if she's not here and you're just being weird, I contractually obligated to beat you up."

"I totally understand, and, yes, she is here."

"Good."

They went up to the seventh floor, and when they got to the room, indeed there was Mrs. Franklington (Eda), who was part Rurulian, and had big white-blonde hair and a creamy smooth pink complexion, a very big bosom and a very small waist, wearing classy but fancy and expensive clothing. Her room looked as if it belonged to a rich harlot, decorated in white and black and red, with red seated stools at their kitchenette.

"Don't tell me you're cheating on me again," she said as soon as she saw him with Tabitha.

"No, ma'am, I am his bodyguard, not remotely his mistress."

Eda laughed. "Not remotely, I like you already."

"I hope this man doesn't come around with mistresses around you or not around you, how dare he?" said Tabitha judgmentally.

"How many children have you had by women that were not me since we've gotten married?" Eda asked George.

"I forget," said George with a humble tilt of his head.

"You see, he forgets how many children he has that aren't mine."

"That's partially because women lead me on to believe that children who are not mine, are mine," said George. "It turns out that I'm quite gullible. It could be zero."

"It's at least four," said Eda. "I've done the DNA testing."

"I'm sorry."

"Wow," said Tabitha. "How dare you treat this sweet and beautiful woman this way?"

"Did you say you have a husband? Does he not cheat on you?"

"No, never," said Tabitha. "Once a drunk lady kissed him, but she kissed him, not visa versa. And so I punched her. That happened yesterday."

"So he does cheat on you."

"No, she did that herself. Stop trying to paint my husband with the same brush as yourself."

"So why is he angry with you, then?"

"Some things should remain private."

"Ah, so you're the cheater."

"I am not a cheater!" Tabitha swore vehemently. "Please stop talking before your cynicism rubs off on me."

Unbeknownst to Tabitha, Frankfurt saw the eviction notice before her and was doing ride-sharing, dressed up as a woman, (because it was illegal for men to pilot broomsticks, which made him feel as if he was fighting for more universal freedom).

"Hey, hey there!" This was Sergeant Marybeth. Of course, she would need a ride somewhere. Did she recognize him? She'd drunkenly kissed him, yesterday. He had mixed feelings about that. Partially he felt violated and some part he wouldn't admit to felt flattered. He wanted to be a better man who wouldn't have enjoyed seeing his wife punch her, but he was very flattered by Tabitha's jealousy.

"Oh, hello," said Frankfurt in a high-pitched voice, looking quite unconvincingly female. "Did you need a ride somewhere?"

"Yes, I need to get to the Rich Harlot, ASAP; there's an emergency there," said Sergeant Marybeth, not recognizing that this was the man she'd drunkenly kissed yesterday. Matter of fact, she didn't even notice that Frankfurt wasn't female. She had her suspicions, but she really didn't care about the sex of her ride sharers.

Sergeant Marybeth was a great friend up until the time when she kissed Frankfurt. She really didn't mean to do that; she was quite drunk at the time. Like that time she kissed Tabitha. She'd also kissed Sergeant Glen before realizing that Sergeant Glen was incorrigible scum. Perhaps the reason why Sergeant Marybeth had so much trouble with men (and she really did have a lot of it) was because she'd been drinking a lot lately and therefore her mind was addled. So, she picked unsuitable men to be her boyfriends, and kept discovering them with other women or getting the "we should see other people" talk. So far, her ex-boyfriend tally for the year was 4.

Frankfurt started getting the idea, what if someone took a picture of him with Sergeant Marybeth at The Rich Harlot? While he needed the money (he saw the eviction notice and that's why he was ride-sharing now), he did not need Tabitha even more angry at him than she already was.

Frankfurt missed her already. How stupid was he to let the fight progress so far that they would agree to take a break! He needed the break to be over with, yesterday. How terrible would it be to show up at his best friend's wedding on a recent break with his wife of nearly twenty years? That was bad luck. He had to make it better for her.

What Tabitha was doing right then was fighting a baboon, and she was beginning to think she had over-estimated her self-defense prowess. Because she was used to fighting with humans, mainly, and fighting a short little guy with razor sharp teeth was a whole new experience. He was very serious about fighting, and Tabitha had that stupid pro-short prejudice where she couldn't assault people smaller than herself, and she was much more used to fighting people that were her size or bigger.

Then she thought about Sergeant Marybeth kissing her husband and pretended the baboon was Sergeant Marybeth. This helped. To think the two of them were friends! Ugh! She still wasn't over being mad about it. If there ever was a moral to that story, it's that you can't kiss your friend's husband and expect her not to get mad about it. Especially in front of her. There's no right way to kiss your friend's husband, but especially not feet away from her. And then Tabitha had to paranoidly wonder if Marybeth had ever done this to Frankfurt before? (She hadn't.)

The fight wasn't going so well. The fact is, baboons are more evolutionarily adapted to hand-to-hand-to-mouth combat than humans are.

"Help!" cried Tabitha, and George and his wife Eda, with Tabitha's help, were able to get Edington tied up with duct-tape.

"Down with the president," Edington chanted, not at all himself.

"Yes, yes, but why down with the president?" asked George, thinking that perhaps he should have listened to Edington's criticisms more closely in the past and then he'd know what this was all about.

"Politicians are evil."

"That is such an un-nuanced worldview."

"Has he always been like this?" asked Tabitha.

Chapter 8

Frankfurt, still wearing his wig and whole female getup, wanted to drop off Sergeant Marybeth slightly away from the Rich Harlot, but unfortunately she talked him into not only dropping her off there, but going with her into the hotel so that after she finished clearing up the emergency, he could take her back to the university, where her precinct was.

"I promise I won't take up too much of your time, and you can keep charging me for the time spent at the hotel..."

Frankfurt had never been more embarrassed in his life, and that's even with having a tail fin that made it so he had to wear altered pants. It's a good thing Tabitha wasn't there, because if she saw him there at a place called The Rich Harlot, she would poop a brick and then throw it at him, metaphorically speaking. Metaphorically speaking, she would beat the ARBOR out of him. Metaphorically speaking, he was very afraid of his wife and had no more metaphors for it.

So, he was very surprised to see his wife in the Rich Harlot with the president and his wife and the president's baboon butler wrapped up in duct tape and taped to the chair.

"Frankfurt, what are you doing here? And with her?"

"Frankfurt?" said Sergeant Marybeth, having not recognized

him until that moment. "Oh, my ARBOR, it's you!"

"Don't play dumb with me, young lady," Tabitha chastised, no longer caring at all that Sergeant Marybeth was a police sergeant. "You can't have my husband."

"I don't want your husband," lied Sergeant Marybeth. Of course, she wanted him; she kissed him yesterday. Why she wanted him was a mystery but maybe one could attribute it to the fact that Frankfurt was a pretty good-looking dude in his own way. She even thought his tail fin was sexy. Not that she would be going for him. She was just very drunk when she'd kissed him, and she thought she was doing Tabitha a favor because apparently Tabitha had kissed someone else (Sergeant Glen) and so Marybeth thought she was doing a good thing by evening the score so that Frankfurt didn't have to be mad at Tabitha anymore. There was a method to her madness. "I'm here to break up the fight and arrest the people involved in it. Which is apparently everybody here."

"No, we're the ones who called the police because this guy here was trying to kill the president and was putting up a freakin' killer fight against me as his bodyguard."

"You're his bodyguard?" asked Frankfurt, stifling a laugh.

"Don't you laugh at me, sir, you are not out of trouble."

"It's just what are you doing here at a hotel with a notorious womanizer, if not being his bodyguard? That is rich."

"Oh, so you don't believe me?"

"I have yet to see you in a fight, ever, and yet apparently you've been fighting a baboon."

"Looks like you all kidnapped him, here," said Sergeant Marybeth.

"I didn't kidnap anybody, we just tied him up so he'd stop trying to kill the president and biting everybody that got in his way." Tabitha lifted her sleeves to show the bitemarks up and down her arms. "Look at what he did to me!"

Frankfurt looked at Tabitha's arms and then looked at Edington dangerously.

"That's my wife!" he yelled.

"And yet here you are here with that harlot who kissed you yesterday."

"I knew he was cheating on you," said George, not helping matters at all.

"You didn't know that because you don't know anything about me and my husband, and if you keep that up, I won't be able to be your bodyguard anymore, because you'll annoy me too much."

"Okay," said Sergeant Marybeth, her mind still addled from her ample alcohol consumption the day before, "who am I supposed to be arresting here?"

Everybody pointed at Edington. "Okay, I'm arresting him for assassination attempt and you three for suspected kidnapping." There was an uproar. "Don't worry, I'll be putting you all in separate cells."

Frankfurt said to Marybeth, "Don't arrest Tabitha."

"I don't want to arrest her, it's just that she's in a very kidnappy situation right now and so we have to get it sorted out before she goes home. It might not even cost you that much."

Tabitha felt truly betrayed. To think she had put aside her fear of the police for this one, only to be arrested by her, the ultimate irony smacking her in the face.

"Do you have the jurisdictional power to arrest the president?" Tabitha asked.

"Oh, that's not the president, stop being specist."

"That is the president. Sir, prove to her that you're the

president."

"I mean, clearly, he is the president," said Frankfurt.

"I am the president," said George. "Of Irrorria, yes, but still an important dignitary here."

"Maybe you can share lawyers with Tabitha because she's your bodyguard," said Marybeth with the air of someone who was being helpful. She winked at Tabitha, while Tabitha thought terrible things about law enforcement.

Tabitha thought quickly. "Um, Sergeant Marybeth, how are you going to get us to the jail?"

"Excuse me?"

"There are four people here who you want to arrest. How are you going to transport all of us?"

She looked at Frankfurt, who shook his head at her. Then she looked at Tabitha who also shook her head at her.

"I mean, what's to stop me from just flying off?"

"I could arrest you at some other time."

"But you won't because you'll find that Edington was trying to assassinate the president and I heroically for money put myself in the way of him so that he wouldn't do it, and there's nothing illegal about self-defense."

"Now hold on a minute, Tabitha..."

But Tabitha got on her broom, followed quickly by the president and the president's wife, and they flew down the hall, being chased by Sergeant Marybeth and not Frankfurt, who was yelling after his wife, "Fly honey fly!" And fly she did, she flew as fast as she could through the fancy hallways with their fancy red carpeted floors with black and white tiles, to the elevator, where they waited patiently for the elevator to get there, and then down the elevator (still hovering patiently), through the lobby, out the doors, and then through the sky. Tabitha decided to stretch her chops as a ride sharing pilot of a stretch broomstick, and flew like a plane into the sky above the clouds. It was a beautiful blue day.

"Oh, honey, this is nice!" said Mrs. Franklington. "I like your ride sharing bodyguard here, she's cool."

"Oh, thank you!" said Tabitha.

"Oh, no, thank you! I've led a very exciting life and this tops everything!"

"I really love my job right now," said Tabitha. "I hope I don't get arrested later."

"I don't know why a nice lady like you would ever get arrested," said Mrs. Franklington (Eda). She put a hand on George's hand, which was around her. Eda looked around, seeing a gorgeous blue day and clouds beneath them as if they were in ARBOR's Haven. It was storming beneath them, somewhat ruining the effect.

"You'd be surprised," said Tabitha. "You're a politician's wife, what's your take on the royals?"

"That's the scariest shit ever," said Eda. "They killed the shit out of them. Terrible tragedy."

"Oh the patriots that did that," said Tabitha with smiling sarcasm. "They come in and kill everybody and say they did a good thing. They were watering the tree of liberty." What she held back was, "With my people's blood."

"Don't tell me you're an anti-royalist?" said Eda. "I thought a servant class such as yourself would like the royals being there."

"Are you guys spies? Are you sent here to find out sensitive information about me so that you can use it to make my life difficult? I feel like there's a lot of that going around recently. Is that paranoia? You guys are high ranking government officials. I bet if I told my psychiatrist about this here, she wouldn't believe me."

"I'm sorry, I'm having trouble keeping up with what you are saying, but no we are not spies. You're very paranoid. You must be a royal. Your secret is safe with me, and definitely George here."

"I'm not a royal, hahahahahahaha, how could you think such a thing? Hahahaha."

"Oh, okay, right, gotcha." And she said no more about it. But it made perfect sense to Eda that Tabitha was a royal because 1) she looked a lot like the queen, and 2) she was obviously bitter about The Terror. Also because she knew how to fight really well, even to hold her own against a murderous baboon (and baboons were just physically better suited to hand-to-hand murder attempting than humans are). That must have been because of the rang phenomenon. Eda just so happened to be really great at deductive reasoning, and her reasoning had led her to a number of correct assumptions that she would be keeping to herself from now on.

Tabitha decided that she liked Eda Franklington. "Since we're on the lamb now, would you two like to accompany me to my best friends' wedding?"

"Oh, that would be lovely," said Eda, "Right George?"

"Oh, yes, honey," said the president, sounding kind of sarcastic, "but now that my assassination attempter is in jail, I think maybe we can let Miss Tabitha go to her friend's wedding on her own without us."

"We'll be like wedding crashers," said Eda.

"We'll be literal wedding crashers, that's so rude."

"Well, you know, we don't have to go to the wedding quite yet, I just need to check up on them and make sure everything is copacetic. I was supposed to give them a ride way earlier than this, but the time keeps getting pushed back for some reason because they're driving themselves crazy probably trying to get ready."

For clarity, Andromedo was not driving himself crazy at all to get ready. He'd gotten ready several hours early and was taking the downtime to go play some videogames and wait for Kelly to be ready to go. That was the hard part, because today was a day when there were a lot of marriages, and the priest was waiting for some time to open up, so to say.

Tabitha was still flying high but got close to their apartment building. One of the funny things about this apartment building was that because it was part-aquatic and out in the sea, there was a lobby on the top floor, as well as one on the bottom in case someone had business to do under the sea. (Business business, you know, not natural business, but sometimes that too.)

When it was time, Tabitha turned at a 30 degree downward angle, through the clouds, into the rain and thunderstorm, and ended up at Andromedo and Kelly's apartment building. They got off the broomstick and walked through the building, down the elevator, with the mouth-pieces (Tabitha had a few extra sets which she always kept on her, just in case), and still, the apartment was full and Kelly was looking like a very beautiful hurricane.

"Oh, hi Tabitha, and I see now the president's wife, Mrs. Franklington…"

"So how goes the wedding proceedings?"

"We're going to need a few hours for a time slot to open up for the nearby preachers, apparently this is a day where a lot of people are trying to get married. I don't get it. It's stormy weather, and we only want to get married today because we're tired of waiting."

"They must be tired of waiting too," said Tabitha unhelpfully.

"Yeah, well, they can be tired of waiting on their own time, because I'm tired of waiting, too and I just want to get married, damn it!" Her voice went shrill and dolphiny for a second, and then she put on a smile again, and said, "It is nice to be meeting the president's wife, though. Do you prefer Eda or Mrs. Franklington?"

"Eda's fine," said Mrs. Franklington.

"How's that assassination attempt going?" asked Kelly.

"Well, we called the police on him when he and I got into a fight, but then Sergeant Marybeth decided to arrest all of us, so we had to fly away."

"Ugh, recently, she is the worst!" said Kelly. "I hate to say it, too, it's like she drank too much at some point and it's making her not smart."

"Yeah, but hopefully Edington the butler is in jail right now and therefore unable to kill me right now," said George.

"Yeah, that's if she managed to keep him in custody while chasing us," said Tabitha. What she didn't know was that Frankfurt had subdued Edington until Sergeant Marybeth was ready to arrest him, so he definitely got arrested. He also negotiated for Tabitha not to get arrested, by saying that he wouldn't fly back Sergeant Marybeth if she did arrest her. There was also a bunch of other stuff she didn't know in the near thereafter.

"You say that Edington the Butler is under mind control drugs?" Kelly asked.

"I think so," said Tabitha.

"I have something for that."

"What–what?"

"Anti–mind–control syringe," said Kelly, handing them a

capped syringe. Tabitha's mouth dropped open. "You're welcome."

Tabitha remembered in the art of potions and spell craft, Kelly excelled at those things, even moreso than Tabitha who never once made a proper potion and who's claim to the label witch came mostly from the fact that she had a broomstick and knew how to fly it.

"I knew we were friends through divine coincidence," said Tabitha, finally. "How many of these do you got? They got Harley, too."

"One can cover maybe three people if you're not worried about germs."

"Oh, I guess I'm going to have to get Harley first with this. And thank you, thank you so much."

"This is going to be a story I tell my grandkids about my wedding day."

"Speaking of, when's that happening?

"It's been delayed until tonight." Then she burst into tears.

"ARE YOU ALRIGHT PRETTY LADY!" Tabitha bounded into a hug with her best friend, and hugged with all of her heart.

"Tabitha, I can't deal right now. I'm having a panic attack. Stop hugging me, no offense, I love you." Tabitha stepped out of the hug, and Kelly drew in a deep breath and fanned her face. "Oh, what am I doing? Marriage is such a big step. I HAVEN'T SEEN ANDROMEDO ALL DAY. Because I'm wearing this stupid beautiful dress, and he's playing videogames, I KNOW HE'S PLAYING VIDEOGAMES, and all I want to do is play videogames with him and he won't let me because he doesn't want to see me in the dress until we're at the altar, WHICH SUCKS THE PRESIDENT'S MAJESTIC BABOON BUTT!"

Andromedo was a loud laugher and they heard him in the other room, laughing happily. A man just about to get married to his soul mate. Then he yelled at some campers in a creative stream of consciousness.

"I can't even," said Kelly.

"So, I just stick them in the jugular with this," said Tabitha holding up the syringe, "and then what?"

"Then the mind control wears off. They actually taught us this one in the witch's apprenticeship, Tabitha. Don't tell me you weren't listening."

"I had no idea I'd ever need it," said Tabitha honestly, having the unfortunate habit of glazing over during a lecture.

"Yeah, life can be crazy sometimes," said Kelly. "I've had to use it on Andromedo a couple of times, now. People are crazy, sometimes they stick others with mind control drugs. You need to be vigilant and prepared if you never want to get used like a pawn in another person's chess game."

"I will pay more attention next time we do continuing magic education," Tabitha swore.

She went off with the president and his wife, again, since the wedding wasn't for a few hours at least. Out to the lobby on top of the apartment building, then onto the broomstick and off and away from the drizzling rain into the bright afternoon sky.

"Drop us off at the Rich Harlot," said Mrs. Franklington, giggling.

"Okay, you two crazy lovebirds," said Tabitha with a snort. She didn't understand the kind of marriage that these two had, but they appeared to be quite fond of each other, so that was nice. If Frankfurt was anything like George, she'd have kicked him to the curb long ago.

As she was flying to The Rich Harlot, the thing she kept thinking was, "Frankfurt better not still be there. If he's still there, I don't know what I'll do. I'll scream. I'll divorce him."

Poor Frankfurt was still there. But not for the reason why Tabitha was thinking he would be there. Shortly after Edington was arrested, he broke free from his constraints, bit everybody within biting distance, and disappeared into the hotel. So now he was there under Sergeant Marybeth's pay to help try to find the baboon.

Tabitha arrived to find Frankfurt in the lobby, looking stupid.

"I knew it!" she yelled, scaring the president and his wife off her broom. "What the hell are you still doing here?"

"What the hell are you still doing here?" yelled Frankfurt, his creativity at a low and because it was a good question.

"I flew the president and his wife back here and will be handsomely compensated!"

"I'm looking for the baboon who tried to kill him and who bit you up, and will be compensated in such a way that is hopefully handsome!"

"Have you located Edington yet?" asked the President, in great worry.

"No, we haven't 'located Edington yet,'" said Frankfurt in such a way that seemed kind of petty. Frankfurt wasn't impressed by the president. Nobody was really impressed by the president, except for Tabitha and she was only slightly impressed with and far from starstruck. It was like the president was just a guy who was kind of short and hairy and very impressed with himself. But it was nice that he was nice to service workers.

"I'm going to die today," said the president.

"You are not going to die today sir!" said Tabitha, in the overly zealous way a person can be when they're getting paid for the service of security. She was getting paid so she was absolutely honor bound to make sure that the president didn't die any time soon. It would bother her now if he did die, which she maybe wouldn't have cared either way yesterday on that account.

The president got out his wallet and pulled several paper monetary notes out to give to Tabitha, and then more to her husband, saying, "That's to pay for you to take your wife to The Rich Harlot. She's been talking about you all day."

"Good stuff, I hope?" said Frankfurt, looking at Tabitha. Tabitha nodded, still looking annoyed at Frankfurt and now the president. Then Frankfurt gave the money back to the president, but Tabitha was like, "No, I can't unhear that so we might as well take advantage of the fool's money. No offense sir."

Tabitha was excited. "I'm going to give this to Kelly and Andromedo for the occasion of their wedding night."

"I thought that was for us," said Frankfurt. "Though I like your idea. I just like it less than the original idea. Which was that we use it. Why don't we turn it into a party room, we have it for all night."

"That sounds splendid. Yes!!! YAASSSS! I don't know if I'm properly conveying what a great idea I think that is."

"We'll see you guys later," said the president, walking off with Eda his wife.

Chapter 9

I haven't done this room at The Rich Harlot justice. It was like something you might see of a rich hotel in a comic book. The walls were bright white and tall, and the furniture was all either red or black. There were long silk gray curtains hanging from the ceiling separating a very large room from the kitchenette area, a sparkling white wine of finest vintage from Whalerian origins (they had the best climate for it). The floors were black and white tiled and immaculately clean as if new.

"That president guy is alright, kind of a creep, but alright otherwise," said Frankfurt. "Let me know if he hits on you so I can punch him in the nose."

"He hasn't hit on me, I wouldn't be working for a guy who hits on me, you know that."

"You're right, I do know that. I think."

"Don't you imply otherwise."

"I wouldn't do that, except the green eyed monster has really been plaguing me recently. I keep thinking about you and that trashy police guy."

"He got fired from the police."

"Ah, that's right, the exotic dancer."

"I paid him extra not to dance."

"You kissed him."

"Yeah, to knock him out, do some witch stuff, escape prison. It's not the same as kissing a guy because you like him. Besides, Sergeant Marybeth kissed you. How long has that been going on for?"

"Literally that was the first last and only time she'll ever do that," said Frankfurt, supremely annoyed.

"Let's drink together," said Tabitha, changing the subject. "But only a little bit because I have to fly tonight."

"Okay!" said Frankfurt, happy for the arguing to be over with. He walked over to the red silk bed (something Tabitha specifically thought that a rich harlot would have such a bed), and sat on it and waited for Tabitha to pour them both wine glasses. The bed sagged in an insanely comfortable way against his weight. For context, Frankfurt's a big dude. He's a nerd who's built like a football player, who then became a dad. Shoulders like a linebacker. And that's not to mention his tail fin.

Okay, let's talk about his tail fin. Frankfurt was part dolphin chimera (1/8th to be exact) and mostly looked like a regular human Gargantuan man, but he also had a dolphin tail fin on his lower back. This invited a lot of mockery in rougher neighborhoods, like where the mangs were at (math gangs, it's a big thing in this series). Tabitha personally thought that his tail fin was sexy. (A lot of women in their world thought that. Tabitha knew.)

She brought him his glass of sparkling Irrorrian wine, along with her own glass, and they clinked glasses (like crystals), and both drank their wine faster than they should have. Tabitha took a flying leap back into the plush silk comforter on the plush silk bed, and handed somewhere towards the middle of the bed (it was a very big bed, much larger than what they were used to, which was a full sized bed.)

Frankfurt looked over at his wife and in his mind a little old man was narrating that this was how Tabitha got pregnant with baby number 6. She looked very pretty against those red sheets, which were particularly complimentary to her bronze, freckled skin and bright blue violet eyes. Though she was technically overweight, she was supermodel beautiful. At least to Frankfurt's eyes.

Suddenly, there was a knocking on their door. Lo and behold, who was it, but Sergeant Marybeth. She was looking as if she'd gotten on the wrong end of a gang fight. Even Tabitha was sympathetic to her plight, looking like that.

"Marybeth, what happened?" asked Tabitha, forgetting for a second that another woman was calling on her husband at a hotel called The Rich Harlot. Marybeth started crying.

"I keep getting bit by that damn baboon!" she said. "We're supposed to be able to handle catching anybody, on the force, but I've caught gangsters more easily than this baboon."

"That's right, I have an anti-mind control syringe," said Tabitha. "If you don't arrest me, you can have it. One third a syringe will do. You can get three people with the potion amount if you're not worried about germs. So you should get Harley first because she's also under mind control and who knows what kind of germs politicians' bffs have."

"I saw Harley earlier," said Sergeant Marybeth, taking the syringe, "she was looking kind of out of it."

"Yup, just stick her in the neck, give her one third of the potion, and she'll be free from mind-control. And then stick Edington the butler in the neck, because surely Harley doesn't have any germs that the butler doesn't got." They didn't know this, but they went with it.

"I need a ride if I'm going to catch up with Harley," said Marybeth. Frankfurt and Tabitha did rock paper scissors to see who got to take the illustrious Sergeant Marybeth to stick Harley in the neck. Tabitha lost, meaning she had to go, which was probably better, anyway, because Tabitha was a better defensive broomstick driver.

"Rock paper scissors go!" they said. Frankfurt had paper. Tabitha had rock.

"Rock paper scissors go!" Frankfurt had rock. Tabitha had scissors.

"Fate would have me be the driver," said Tabitha pompously. "Never send a man to do a woman's job, they say, though I'm sure you would rock at it, honey."

"What does that even mean, never send a man to do a woman's job, that's like, 'Never send a man to give literal birth because nothing will happen.' Speaking, of I should go too so that you have backup."

"It is like that. Well, I guess I'll go get Harley with you."

Marybeth said, "I'm sorry about yesterday and this morning, I don't know what's gotten into me."

"I do, you've got a case of the shouldn't haves for my husband."

"That's not true."

"I know you, and your taste in men is super-bad and it must be to try to get my super-nice man from me, your friend, that's an example of having bad taste in men."

"I don't know whether to be complimented or insulted," said Frankfurt. "It doesn't matter, honey, because you are the only one for me and no other woman could even momentarily distract me from you."

"I don't want to steal your man from you," said Marybeth. "Drunk me thought that since you kissed the former sergeant Glen, that I would make things even for you by kissing Frankfurt."

"See, that doesn't even make any damn sense. Maybe you were trying to make the former sergeant jealous, and I can see Frankfurt being the most handsome option around, but you're going to have to back off, there."

"I am totally backed off."

"Good. I forgive you."

"I forgive you too."

"I haven't done anything wrong."

"Let's not ruin the moment."

It wasn't long after being in the sky that Harley popped up behind them, with Edington the Butler on the back of her broom.

"Let me do this," said Frankfurt.

"Do what?"

"Let me stick them in the neck with the syringe."

"Oh, you want to do that? Good, because I did not want to do that."

"Okay, now that that's settled," Frankfurt flew off in the direction of their aerial enemies. First he got the Butler in the neck (because the Butler was the one giving him the most trouble) and then he got Harley in the neck. Then everybody landed to see how this worked out.

"Oh, wow, what happened?" asked Edington, rubbing his neck.

"You tried to kill the president and bit everybody who got in your way and threw a knife or kunai or something wrapped in poop," Tabitha explained as gently as she could.

"I am so sorry!" said Edington, not a guy who was used to apologizing. "Where's George? Does he hate me now?"

"He's not here," said Tabitha, "but I think he pretty well accepts that you were under mind control drugs. And this proves it because..." she prompted.

"I no longer want to kill the president. I never actually wanted to kill him. We joke around sometimes about me killing him, but that was a joke. Oh ARBOR!"

"Stop freaking out, this is a good thing," said Tabitha.

"You know, that mind control stuff makes a lot of sense now that I think about it now," said Harley, stepping off of her broom. She looked at Frankfurt. "Did you jab me in the neck with the same syringe you used on Edington?"

"Um, yes, sorry about that," said Frankfurt. "I had to take care of the biggest threat first. The plan was to jab you in the neck, first, but you weren't the biggest threat and I had to make a split second judgment call."

"Why not just use two syringes?"

"We only had one."

"That's unsanitary. I'm glad I got my cooties shot, but I'm not even sure if it's going to do anything now that I've been jabbed in the neck with someone else's needle." She looked at Edington. "Be honest, I know this is a touchy subject, but do you have the cooties?"

"I don't have the cooties," said Edington. "I got my cooties shot."

"I got it too."

"Thank ARBOR," they both said.

Chapter 10

“Oh, it’s only the beginning of the day, and I am bone tired,” said Tabitha, meeting back up with Frankfurt at their hotel room for the night.

“You’re telling me! I had no idea the first part of a day of ride sharing would be so exciting.”

“Too exciting, if you ask me. All I ever wanted was a responsible life, none of that terrible excitement nonsense,” lied Tabitha. Logically she wanted a boring life, but emotionally, she dug excitement.

“Oh, don’t lie, you were having a great time,” said Frankfurt.

“I mean, yes, when I wasn’t getting bit by a crazed on drugs baboon, I was having a pretty good time.”

“What do you think about that president guy?”

“He’s nice to service workers, but he doesn’t understand the sorts of things one should and shouldn’t say around us. Kind of a creep but I have met bigger creeps. And I like that he bought us a hotel room, despite that he was probably doing that to make up for directly insinuating to me that you were cheating on me.”

“Classic projection. He cheats on his wife so he thinks everybody cheats on their wife.” He noticed Tabitha looking petulant so he said, “Come here, you.”

She came to him and he hugged her and kissed her deeply. Passionate, she climbed on top of him, when her cell phone beeped again. It was the Broomr app, letting her know that her favorite old ladies needed a ride...

"At this time of the day?" questioned Tabitha. "They usually want me to pick them up at two or three in the morning." Tabitha sighed deeply and loudly.

"Go make that money, honey," said Frankfurt. "I'll ride share too until we get that house note paid."

"What are you ladies doing out so early in the day?" asked Tabitha, picking up her favorite trio of old ladies, Mrs. Pringelle, Mrs. Donnell, and Mrs. Jones. Usually they were dressed in sexy party clothes, but today, they were dressed all in black. "Funeral?"

"Yes," said Mrs. Pringelle, "Our friend Walter died recently. Your friend Harley got our husbands."

"Wow, she does not stop to take a break ever," said Tabitha. Normally, she was used to doing this work at night, but she was making a killing today working in the day.

"Did you know that we were going to a funeral because you're a witch?" asked Mrs. Jones.

"No, I guessed it because you all were wearing black," admitted Tabitha.

"Smart girl," said Mrs. Jones. All three women were wearing big sunglasses, something that Tabitha thought that she should have remembered.

They loaded onto her broom and she took them on a thirty-degree angle into the sky, keeping low because she didn't want them falling off of her broom. Tabitha once had a bad experience of getting a faller and never forgot it. The rain beaded over their force-field without hitting any of them, though the old women also brought umbrellas.

"Oh, can't you go over the clouds?" asked Mrs. Donnell, "It's such a dreary day."

"Okay," said Tabitha, and flew over the clouds to the wonderland that was Gargantua's skies in the middle of the day during a storm.

"Oh, this is nice!" said Mrs. Pringelle, the other old ladies agreeing.

"Yeah, flying above the clouds is pretty sweet, but aren't you all's ears popping?"

"We chew gum for these trips."

Every once in a while, a customer would get motion sickness (they called it sky sickness), and Tabitha's faller was also a puker. She caught him but he broke a toe pretty badly. Pukers made her very nervous for this reason, also because it was most likely that even if the customer didn't directly puke on her, puke would land on her anyway because of the wind.

People also sometimes complained of ear popping. Most people wanted her to fly low. Trust these sweet old ladies to want Tabitha to fly high. Then came the problem that the funeral was right under the stormiest part of the cloud.

"I can't fly through that," Tabitha informed them. "Too dangerous. I don't know how lightning will affect my forcefield around us."

"It's too bad about those lightning rods around ARBOR's church/power station," said Mrs. Pringelle.

"I'll just fly around the storm and go under that way," said Tabitha. She flew her stretch broomstick in the direction of some whiter clouds, and then went under to an overcast day, into the storm. It was still raining heavily. Finally, they arrived at The

First Temple/Power station of ARBOR, where three little old men were waiting on them. Tabitha thought, "Those are goals," to be married to a little old Frankfurt at that age. (Frankfurt needed to cooperate by eating right, but he seemed to think he was impervious to poor eating choices, so Tabitha countered that as best as she could by leaving very healthy food in the house as the staple.)

'It's too bad about Walter," said Mr. Pringelle.

"He had at least another good ten years in him," said Mr. Jones.

"Pfft, ten, at least twenty," said Mr. Jones.

This was Tabitha's first time meeting The Trio's husbands. She had been giving them rides for ARBOR knows how long now, and this was her first time seeing them. They were very old, like their wives, and dressed in their finest black suits.

The First Temple/Power station of ARBOR, was exactly what it sounded like; part temple, part power station for the community. Through its lightning rods, it stored more than enough electricity to keep the township going indefinitely. You couldn't tell it was a power station from the inside, though, which looked like a typical Arborian temple with stained glass windows depicting all of the heroic deeds of ARBOR. Not all of them were power stations, though many Arborian temples were power stations because they were very tall and therefore good for lightning rods.

"Well, I guess I better get going then," said Tabitha, and they paid her for her services. She was about to leave when a masked gunman entered the temple, and shouted, "Everybody on the floor, and give me all of your money!"

"Wow, a robbery at a funeral," Tabitha thought. "Just when you thought you've seen everything."

Tabitha had a lot of money on her at this point. That was rent money. Who the hell did this robber think that he was, thinking he was going to be taking her money? She laid down on the floor, thinking these dangerous thoughts.

Tabitha had two fathers. One was biological (the guy who didn't raise her) and one wasn't (the guy who raised her). And both of them thought that ride sharing was too dangerous for her. She never agreed with either of them, and yet today, she'd fought off an assassin and was present for a temple robbery. As a nonreligious person, it logically made sense to her that sometimes the temple would get robbed, just because the tithers kept the temple having lots of money. It's just not something she thought would happen; she was sure that her people were too superstitious to do such a thing. Even being nonreligious, she was too superstitious to do such a thing. She didn't have the right kind of constitution to be a professional criminal; she enjoyed her freedom too much for that. That and she had a heart problem that made her heart beat way too fast if she could potentially be in trouble.

Her heart was beating like that now. She tried to breathe, to make sure that she didn't have a heart attack. She quietly chanted a calming spell on her heart, slowing it down and making it easier for her to breathe.

"You there!" said the criminal, talking so loudly and directly at Tabitha that she had to look at him. "Witch! I know you have money."

"How can he tell I'm a witch?" thought Tabitha, and then realized she was still holding her broomstick. "I have no money!" she said loudly to him.

"Witch, I saw you get money from those old ladies."

"That's to keep a roof over the heads of my family and

children, so it's not for you," said Tabitha. "I have no money for you."

They had done a class on this in the witch's apprenticeship. Most service industries, if you got robbed, they just wanted you to absorb the loss, but being a witch was different. A large part of what made a witch a witch in this world, was that they were supposed to be intimidating. Tabitha was actually pretty good at that part. She was so good at cursing people that her kids kept reminding her to stop doing it, because she had a problem of feeling guilty afterwards.

She wondered if she would feel guilty cursing someone with a gun to her head,

"Witch, do you want to die?"

She didn't quite stand up so much as levitate up. It was a dangerous thing to anger a witch; levitation was more of a symptom of the problem. The problem was that a witch was severely feeling some kind of way. You could tell from the levitation. Another thing that might have given it away were the whites of her eyes, which were the only parts of her eyes that were visible at that time.

"Oh," said the robber, along with some choice words, "I wasn't expecting that." And he shot at her, but the bullets hit the force-field around her and fell to the ground.

"This is your first time trying to rob a witch, isn't it?" asked Tabitha, deceptively gentle. The robber nodded fearfully. "Okay, then, give me all of your money."

"What? That's not how it works."

"That is how it works when you rob a witch. Give me all of your money or I'll curse you with the cooties and your face will fall off."

"Cooties is a virus, you can't curse someone to get it!" yelled the robber in a panic.

"Watch me," said Tabitha. "This is going to be the least guilty I ever feel over any curse."

"Just take the money!" yelled the robber, giving her his impressive cash stash.

"Thank you so much," said Tabitha, pocketing her newly earned money. "Now your gun."

"I have to give you my gun, really?" said the robber, now in a foul mood.

"If you don't want your face to fall off, you definitely have to give me your gun," said Tabitha resolutely. The robber sourly gave her his gun. She put it in her witch's pocketbook, feeling extra rich today. Then she realized that she was the one with the gun, so she took it out of her pocketbook and said, "Now you get on the floor."

"Really?!"

"Really." She pointed the gun at his face. The robber was so distraught that tears leaked out of his eyes. She put the gun closer to him and pulled the hammer. He got on the floor.

"Well, everybody," she said, "The rest of you can get up except for this robber here. He has to stay on the floor and do penance to ARBOR for trying to rob a funeral in His house. I have to go."

There was a round of applause for Tabitha as she left the funeral, and the temple monk began the funeral processions.

Chapter 11

"Wow, will this day ever end?" Tabitha asked herself as she flew back to her picking up people point. It had been the longest of long days. First it started with Frankfurt and her breaking up. Then there was the eviction notice. Then was her epic adventure with the president of Irrorria. And intimidating that robber. All the back and forth to Kelly's apartment.

She decided that this would be a good time to inform Kelly of their hotel room win. She dialed her number.

"Hello?" answered Kelly, sounding harried.

"Hi pretty lady," said Tabitha, "the president got us a hotel room for the night and we thought it would be better to go to you and Andromedo."

"Say what?"

"The president gave me and Frankfurt a ticket to stay at the Rich Harlot hotel, but we're not the ones getting married, so we decided to rent the room for you and Andromedo."

Kelly sounded moved by this gesture. "Really, Tabitha?"

"Are you okay with that?" Tabitha asked. "Because if not we can..."

"I'm okay with it!" she interjected.

"Oh, good."

"We still don't know when the wedding's going to take place, though," said Kelly sadly.

"I'm sorry."

"Don't be; it's not your fault." She yawned deeply. "I'm thinking we might do the wedding tomorrow."

"Whenever you two do the wedding, we'll be there," Tabitha vowed. She heard some sniffling on the other end of the phone. "What's wrong?"

"I'm just feeling extra emotional, with this wedding coming up," Kelly cried.

"It's a beautiful thing that you two are getting married," said Tabitha. "I can't think of two people more meant for each other."

"Are you and Frankfurt okay?"

"Pfft, we can't stay mad at each other long," said Tabitha. "We already made up earlier today."

"What's been going on with Sergeant Marybeth?"

"She apologized to me. I suppose it makes it even that she kissed Frankfurt, because she kissed me, before, too."

"What? No!"

"Hahaha, yeah, she was drinking heavily on that day, too."

"I feel like there's a cautionary tale in here about drinking too much alcohol."

"Yeah, I see it too. It's a good thing she doesn't have the cooties, or both of our faces would have fallen off."

"Ooh, pretty lady, you can't be too careful nowadays."

"You're telling me."

"So what's the number at the Rich Harlot hotel?"

"Room 312 on the third floor," Tabitha told her.

"We'll be there."

Tabitha got off the phone with Kelly and flew her broom into the sky above the clouds, to get some fresh air. She took down the force field for a moment and just took some time flying through the sky, her hair wild around her, to appreciate the feeling of the high sky in the middle of the day. Then she reinstated the force field and flew back into the rain. Her cell phone dinged again, and she looked at the Broomr app to realize that she had more people waiting on her, this time at the airport. So she flew to the airport, feeling very important today. After all, what could top flying around the president of Irrorria, thwarting an assassination, and a robbery attempt? It had been a most eventful day!

The couple waiting on her were these skinny whisps of people. The woman had beige-gray hair and large eyes, and the man looked kind of like maybe Frankfurt would have, if he had spent his life on the brink of starvation. Their bellies were full, meaning that they had eaten recently, which took the edge off of some of Tabitha's shock at seeing such emaciated people.

"Hello! Where to!" asked Tabitha jovially, determined not to comment on their state of emaciation except to politely offer food at some point. They climbed on her broom.

"We're new here," said the woman. Her name was Molly. You might recognize her from the other books, if you've read them. If not, no judgment. "So we really have no idea where to go."

"I'm looking for my father," said the man, whose name was Benny. "He was a professor of calculus."

"Oh," said Tabitha, her stomach turning when she thought of the Genocide of the Maths, "you mean your father survived the purge?"

"He did. We're also survivors of the purge. We were in Irrorria's math camp for the longest time, but that exploded a while back and we've been wandering around ever since. Spent some time in Whalery. That was nice, but they forcibly vaccinate you."

"Those cooties are no joke," said Tabitha. "I knew a guy with cooties and his face fell off."

"That's what we keep hearing. Still, it's my body, so it should be my choice if I want to get vaccinated or not."

"I agree with you to a certain extent," said Tabitha diplomatically, "but cooties are very contagious, so I really don't mind the mandatory vaccinations. Because for all it's problems, I like my face."

"I like your face too," said Molly, and the two women giggled.

"I like your face too," said Tabitha. "The both of you have very nice faces."

She was already fantasizing about cooking these two a veggie lasagna.

"You two must have not had a decent meal in a long time, coming from the math camp," she ventured.

"Oh, we ate okay at the refugee camp in Whalery," said Molly. "But they kicked us out because *somebody* didn't want his cooties shot."

"They gave it to me anyway," said Benny. "I had a rash for two days."

"Hey, it's better than your face falling off," said Tabitha. Benny grunted. "Anyway, I ask because it is my compulsion every time I see anyone as skinny as you two, to offer them a home-cooked meal."

The couple perked up a little at hearing that. "Do you feed your vegetables human remains?" asked Molly. "Because that would really disagree with our stomachs, don't ask me how I know that."

"No, all of my vegetables are bought from a guy called ARBOR like the god," said Tabitha. "He can magic them from nothing. He's also a meat salesman, but who eats meat anymore, right?"

"Right, ew meat," said Molly. "There's nothing more unappealing than the flesh of another sentient being."

"I've got a kickass veggie lasagna to put in the oven later, if y'all are interested," said Tabitha. "I'm sure my husband won't mind me bringing over company."

"Hey, if it's alright with you, it's alright with us," said Benny. "I haven't had a lasagna in decades."

"You wouldn't happen to be part dolphin would you?" asked Tabitha.

"How did you know?" asked Benny.

"Well, you seem to have a dolphin fin on your lower back, and my husband's part dolphin so he has that too."

"Really?"

"Yes, he's an attractive man and it's one of his better qualities."

"I never met anybody outside of my family with a dolphin fin on his lower back," said Benny thoughtfully.

"Yeah, it's pretty rare," said Tabitha. "Unfortunately, he catches a lot of hell over it. Hecklers will say things to him like, 'Damn boi, that tale is thick! With two c's!' And, 'Shake that tale, baby.'"

"Oh, don't even," said Benny. "I got enough of that at the camp."

"I had no idea there was any other guy in the world that went through that. You look kind of like him, too."

"I look like your husband?"

"Like a version of him that's not been well-fed at all." A pause. "What's your last name?"

"Walker," they both said, since Molly considered herself to be Benny's common-law wife, which meant adopting his last name.

"Hey! I'm a Walker, too!" said Tabitha. "Maybe we're related through marriage."

"Maybe."

"So since you all don't know where you're going, I'll just take you home and introduce you to the family, and if you're a relative to us, well, then, you've found where you're going."

"Are your people mathematicians, too?"

"It's too soon to admit to that," said Tabitha. "Decriminalization's only recently taken place, and they still write tickets for math affiliation."

"Hey, at least you don't hate mathematicians," said Molly.

"Of course not, I feel nothing but pity for mathematicians given their historically recent plight." She took a chance and said, "And the royals. It was a horror what they did to them."

"Yeah, poor royals," said Molly. "Real riches to rags situation there."

"For the lucky ones," said Tabitha. "It's better to be poor than it is to be dead."

"That's true," said Benny. A beat. "We got a paycheck from the Whalerian government and decided on a whim to come here to find my family."

"Our family," corrected Molly.

"That's right, our family, sorry about that," said Benny.

"I wish the government gave me paychecks," said Tabitha. "Then I would be a stay-at-home mom which has always been my dream. Don't get me wrong. I really love flying a broom for a living. But it can get tiring. Just today, I thwarted an assassination, got bit real bad by a baboon chimera (nothing against them, it's just what happened), and then thwarted a robbery. This isn't ladies' work."

"I don't know, it sounds like a lot of fun to me," said Molly. Tabitha smiled warmly.

"Gurl, if you think so, you need to join the witch's union. There's an apprenticeship and you learn so much. And there are so many job opportunities awaiting a trained witch."

"You are speaking my language right now," said Molly. "If you don't mind me asking, why would you want to be a stay-at-home mom when you have such an exciting job?"

Tabitha thought about it for a while. "All the excitement wears a person down after a while. I almost got arrested today, and it's not the first time. Having a new witch at the university attracts the attention of the police. They say you don't have to fear the police if you're not doing anything wrong, but some of us were born the wrong way."

"I knew it!" said Benny. Tabitha looked back at him briefly and he said, "Sorry, I was thinking about something else.

It was at that point that Harley pulled up, looking a mix of supremely apologetic and also mildly pissed off, with Glen on the back of her broom.

"Pull over!" said Glen.

Glen was a former sergeant of the police department. Last she saw of him (yesterday), he was an exotic dancer. Who pulls over for an exotic dancer? Tabitha laughed and flew faster.

"Fly faster!" Glen said to Harley. Harley sighed and flew faster. When she got next to Tabitha again, she shrugged and put her hand to her heart, as if to apologize for the inconvenience. "Pull over!" he said again.

"You're an exotic dancer!" Tabitha yelled at him, flying as fast as she could. "Nobody ever has to pull over for you, ever again!"

Benny and Molly burst into nervous laughter. They were afraid they were done for.

Harley said, "Tabitha, I'm sorry I keep getting this guy."

And Tabitha said, "Don't worry, hon, I got this."

See, their friendship was stronger than the coincidence of whomever happened to be on the back of their broom. Tabitha and Harley had been friends for a little over a year, and they were best friends. Harley was also best friends with Kelly, and maybe even better best friends with her. And that was okay, because Tabitha recognized that maybe Harley filled in a part of Kelly's life that Tabitha could not fill. She felt mildly jealous from time to time, but she was also happy for their friendship. Her own friendship with Harley was quite close (as close as she could get with another woman, considering how much she worked, and that she was always watching kids when she wasn't working).

Tabitha flew again in loop-de-loops and all kinds of crazy ways, Benny and Molly screeching with wild scary joy and holding on tight, and, more for fun and payment than anything else, Harley kept up with her as best as she could, knowing that the two of them would reminisce over this later.

"I'm not an exotic dancer anymore!" shouted Glen. "Well, I am one, but I'm also a cop again. The police precinct would fall apart without me."

Tabitha had had quite enough of Glen. Through her long history with him, she had kissed him a few times to bewitch him to fall asleep, and of course he thought that meant that they had had sex together. Long story short, they hadn't. But it still put a serious strain on their marriage. She had kissed him to escape from captivity and certain death, but she still felt like she would have felt some kind of way if Frankfurt had to kiss some woman to escape from captivity and certain death. Granted, she would have easily forgiven Frankfurt for such a thing, even if she wasn't guilty of it herself, because she'd rather have an alive and imperfect Frankfurt than a dead perfect version of him, but, long story short, Glen nearly broke up her marriage because he kept imprisoning her so she could kiss him to escape.

It's perhaps time to explain exactly how these escapes worked. Tabitha would kiss Glen and amidst her kissing him, she would place a sleeping spell on him, and give him wild dreams about having sex with her, and while he was sleeping, she would escape. When he woke up, he would think that the two of them had done sex, but in actuality, he was kissed and then put to sleep. This wasn't a good idea for his ego, so he went with that they had sex, and he believed it. In his mind, Tabitha was with the wrong man, and if only he could prove it to her, then she would leave Frankfurt for him. In Tabitha's mind, and in reality, this would never happen. She loved Frankfurt, and regretted ever having to kiss anybody that wasn't him.

And in all fairness, did she really have to kiss him? Couldn't she have just knocked him out? It was more discreet to kiss him first, and kept him on her better side, but the older she got, the more she realized, she should have just knocked him out. Having him hanging around like a hungry puppy dog hoping to get a treat, certainly did her no favors in the long run. She made a mental note, where he ever to arrest her again, to just knock him out without kissing him. And maybe if she was to put anything in his mind, it would be him having sex with someone weird, since he was always trying to go there with her.

"I don't stop for exotic dancers!" Tabitha yelled at him. She and Harley shared a look; she winked at Harley, and Harley winked back at her. Then she dove the broomstick towards the ground at a negative 20 degree angle as fast as she could, lifting away from the ground at five feet from the ground. Harley stayed where she was, to Glen's enragement.

"Follow her!" Glen yelled, outraged.

"My broom stalled," Harley explained to him. "I need to put it in the shop to get checked out."

"Brooms don't stall! People stall!"

"My broom stalled."

Though it was the second time in the day that Tabitha found herself in a showdown with Harley, she was deeply grateful to her friend. She knew that earlier today Harley was under mind control! Without the mind control, she wouldn't even help the police to catch her.

When things finally calmed down and Harley and Glen were nowhere to be seen, Molly said, "That guy looked strangely familiar."

Benny said, "He looked like that guy Agnes tried to kill back in Irrorria."

Tabitha said, "Well, he was in Irrorria lately and he did come back looking pretty messed up."

There was a long moment of silence before Benny said, "Thank you for not stopping for him."

"Was he the guy that Agnes tried to kill?" Tabitha asked with some amusement.

"Maybe."

Chapter 12

Sergeant Glen had been really having some bad days recently to the point where his inner psychopath and his outer psychopath were one. It wasn't every day someone got brained by an old lady and then by her again and then by that guy on the other broomstick. He'd mock-strangled Molly and that was to escape the murderous household. Karma was coming for him and he knew it and didn't care because getting revenge in a situation like this was definitely not one of the worst things he'd done nor was going to do.

And to think he was the hero who'd liberated that mamp (math camp) for a handsome sum. What a complicated man. He was sitting on the back of Harley's broom and was growing tired of her insolence.

Author's note:

I know Sergeant Glen is a police officer and he's absolutely despicable, and you might read that and think, "This author is anti-police." That simply is not true. It's just that the character is more interesting as a scumbag than he would have been as a good guy. Also because he's the villain. And what scarier job for a villain to have than police officer? He's also a psychological operative.

The seeds of this come from my mental illness. I could talk about it for hours. And you might be entertained.

Okay, so he was sitting on the back of the broomstick and growing tired of Harley's insolence.

"No, she told us about you and you are not going to harass my friend!" yelled Harley, scared out of her wits and half–hoping he would harass her instead. (For all his problems, he was very handsome and she had seen his lookalike brother Sven nearly nude.)

"Harley, it has been a trying time for me. So I hope you forgive me for doing what I'm about to do."

"What's that?"

He stuck her in the neck with a needle and syringe, and pushed the contents of the syringe into her neck.

"What in the name of the Irrorrian president's majestic baboon butt did you put into my neck?" Harley yelled, terrified now.

"I've put you under my mind control."

Harley tried to fight it but ended up saying, "I'm under your mind control."

"You will follow Tabitha wherever she's going, and let me on and off of the broom as I please."

"I will follow Tabitha wherever she's going and let you on and off of the broom as you please."

"Yes, thank you, you're also not charging me for this trip."

"I am not charging you for this trip."

This mind control drug, Wimbish, was effective whether you were a genius or a feeble minded person. It worked on everybody. Harley was quite smart, but under the influence of Wimbish she was completely under the spell of the drug. Otherwise she would have charged the shit out of Sergeant Glen, her unconscious mind reminded her never to give this man a ride again.

"Now go find Tabitha."

Chapter 13

Tabitha made a stop at her house with Benny and Molly, to see if there was anybody home who could confirm their familial affiliation. Out of all five kids, only Marissa was home, and it seemed that Frankfurt was still out.

"Where is everybody?" asked Tabitha.

"They all are out with Grandpa but I had to stay home to do homework because there's a lot of it," said Marissa. "Also, I wish I was a boy."

"Say what?" said Tabitha. "Why do you wish you were a boy?"

"Always have it's just a thing," said Marissa. "I hope you still love me."

"Of course, considering we have magic this is a nothing-burger," said Tabitha, and to prove herself on this she said an incantation and Marissa turned into a boy. "I hope you don't mind. I'll turn you back when you're ready."

Marissa was delighted. "I don't know if I'll ever be ready to turn back now." And he disappeared into the bathroom.

"Wow, you guys, she was so excited that she didn't even notice y'all were here," said Tabitha to Benny and Molly, who were a little bit in awe over the quick display of magic.

"What if she never wants to turn back?" said Molly, who

hadn't even realized that was something that could be done. (The more and more she thought about it, the more she wanted to take Tabitha up on her offer of joining the witch's apprenticeship through the witch's union.)

Tabitha shrugged. "The great thing about being a witch's child is having more options than the children of non-witches. Though it would be a shame for a young lady with such a pretty face to spend her existence as a man. I can't imagine what these men go through, not being able to fly broomsticks and such. But it's my job as mom to be supportive so if she wants to be a boy, now she can experience that."

Frankfurt was a rule breaker and flew a broom anyway because you couldn't tell him he couldn't do something just because of something as stupid as how he was born. That's why he wore a wig and pretended to have a hormonal issue that he was very sensitive about.

Marissa emerged from the bathroom again. "Mom! I've decided on my boy's name. I want to be called Wilbert."

"Okay Wilbert," said Tabitha, trying to suppress a laugh over what she thought was a goofy name.

"What's so funny about that?" asked Wilbert.

"It's just kind of a funny name, which is nice."

A beat. "There's a guy here who looks like dad and a lady who looks like she needs food. They both look like they need food. Would you guys like some food?"

Gargantuan hospitality was supposed to be a real big thing; like the Gargantuans were supposed to be the most hospitable of all the people of their world, but that was also a highly contested claim to fame from other localities.

Molly said, "At this time in my life, I never say no to food."

Benny said, "That would be lovely."

Tabitha got to cooking. What a productive day she was having! Worked hard, got a second gig, protected a president from assassination, got on the run from a dirty cop and from a regular one, magicked her daughter into a son (Frankfurt was going to have a heart attack, none of them knew the extent of her powers), and was now cooking a big meal for everybody. Not to make you, the reader, jealous of the meal that they had, ARBOR bowls of various vegetables and noodles, as well as brownies for dessert, but it was quite good. She set out some plates for everybody there and covered the other plates.

They sat at the table.

"So you two are from a mamp?" asked Wilbert.

"Yes," said Benny and Molly.

"How did you escape?"

"Funny, one day, there were several explosions and we just got out of there as quickly as we could," said Benny, leaving out the part where he and Molly enjoyed their newfound privacy for a few.

"We were in Whalery when that happened," said Tabitha. "Whalery is right next to Irrorria," she explained to Wilbert, purposelessly because Wilbert already knew that thanks to his public-school education, which was purported bad but not so bad as the kids graduated not knowing basic things (except math, but geography was safe). "And we were on our way to Irrorria, but someone beat us to the punch on what we were supposed to do, so we came home."

"What were you on the way to do?" asked Molly.

"Never mind, it'll sound stupid now that it's already done."

"They were supposed to liberate a mamp," said Wilbert. Tabitha sighed.

"It's the thought that counts," said Benny, touched. "What

were you going to do?"

"Blow it up in strategic places."

"That's pretty much exactly what happened."

"That's true, and it was a great thing, the only difference was that we weren't the ones to do it. So we're only wannabe heroes in this case."

"I'm surprised to learn that there's resistance against the mamp movement," said Molly.

"It's very secretive," said Tabitha, "and if y'all were spies you'd already have gotten me."

"We're not spies."

"Most of the time, people don't believe me when I see a spy, but I'm better at spotting them than I'm given credit for. And you two don't ring those bells for me."

"I would rather die than to be that kind of spy," said Benny. He thought about it for a moment, recalling a distant youth where the kids were encouraged to rat each other out at any sign of math-doing. He felt sorry for the young people involved, even though that was the reason why he went to the mamp, due to the moral compromise.

They finished off their meal and Tabitha asked Wilbert where his father was.

"He's with Andromedo and Kelly at The Rich Harlot," said Wilbert, with a laugh.

"Oh, that's okay," said Tabitha, knowing 1) she could trust Frankfurt and 2) she could definitely trust him with Kelly and Andromedo. "Do you mind if I take our dinner guests to go see him?"

"Go ahead, I think Dad'll be tickled that you found someone who looks so much like him," said Wilbert.

"Do you want me to change you back into Marissa, yet?" asked

Tabitha.

"No, Mom, I like the way I am right now," said Wilbert.

"Okay, well, let me know."

"I'll let you know, but I think I'd rather just be like this forever afterwards."

"Okay, that's fine."

She took Benny and Molly on her broomstick and flew into the city to the Rich Harlot.

Frankfurt was on his own at The Rich Harlot, when Andromedo and Kelly arrived, smiling like they had won the lottery.

"This must have been exorbitantly expensive," said Kelly, looking like a movie star, looking around to take in the whole view of this exorbitantly expensive hotel room.

"Not for us!" said Frankfurt. "Lucky for you all, Tabitha's boss is a generous creep who paid for us to have a hotel room after having accused me of cheating. Can you imagine?" He pretended to be George. "I'm the president of a country and I go to some other country and accuse my Broomr driver's husband of cheating on her. I'm a big creep." He thought about it. "Or a little one in his case."

"Hey, but he paid for this fine hotel room," said Andromedo, his eyes locking on the bed, and he took a running leap and jumped to it and slid almost off the bed but not quite. Then he got up again and said to Frankfurt, "Can't be that bad. I could be friends with such a guy. Except his mamp stance."

"Ooh, baby," said Kelly, "apparently he paid for that mamp to be liberated."

"Pfft, okay, I'm sure he did that and didn't just tell you he did that for political reasons."

"I can't vote for him, sweetheart. I live in another country."

"I'm just saying if you could vote for him, thinking that he'd blown up a mamp, letting everybody free, would secure your vote. Unless you were a math hater, in which case, we can't get married."

"I can beat you at math and you know it," said Kelly, who was smarter than the rest of their friends, even at math.

There were things that were illegal in their world that made perfect sense to be illegal. Murder, for example, was illegal. And the people took that law very seriously; murder did take place, but it wasn't common. Math was one of those things that didn't make much sense to be illegal, other than it was purportedly an abomination of ARBOR. This was iffy, because the ARBOR everybody actually interacted with, was not a guy who believed in abominations, much. He had a short list of Actual Abominations: landfills, cooties, pollution, child abuse. Math was not on that list. ARBOR felt that the Math Camps (Mamps) were an abomination. He also would have done the Royal Purge differently. If he was up to changing the government, nobody would have died. But nobody, nobody but as a true ARBOReon.

"I should get going," said Frankfurt, sensing that he was a third wheel.

"Well, it was nice seeing you," said Andromedo, smiling from ear to ear. (The only thing that could have made this better was if this was an underwater level of The Rich Harlot, but alas, they had no underwater levels.)

"Bye now," said Frankfurt, and opened the door to run into Tabitha, Benny, and Molly. "Why hello!" He did a double take when he saw Benny, and then burst into happy tears and gave Benny a big hug. To be hospitable, he gave Molly a hug, too, so it was a group hug. Tabitha didn't want to be left out, so she came in on the hug.

"It's a group hug!" Andromedo announced, and joined the hug, Kelly joining last.

"Nice to meet you," Andromedo said when the hug ended. "You must be Frankfurt's brother; you two look uncannily alike."

"I am," said Benny. "My name is Benjamin Walker, and this is my common law wife Molly Walker."

"We're going to get bona fide married one day," said Molly. "We just haven't had the opportunity yet."

"We're getting married tomorrow," said Kelly.

"Tomorrow?" asked Tabitha. "For some reason, I thought it was going to be sometime tonight."

"There just aren't enough preachers available for tonight so we'll be getting married tomorrow."

"That's fine."

It was at this point that Harley and Sergeant Glen arrived at the hotel room's door. There was a knocking.

Andromedo paled. "Did you tell anybody else about the hotel room?"

Frankfurt had the same look of apprehension. "I didn't. Did you, Tabitha or Kelly?"

Both women shook their heads.

"Open up, it's the police!"

The room went from relatively full to quite empty looking in seconds. Everybody dove behind or under something. Andromedo, being quite tall, hid behind some curtains, with Kelly. Nobody answered the door.

"Open that door," Glen told Harley, who was still under his mind control. Harley, using magic, opened the door and they walked into the room. It was eerily silent.

"It doesn't look like anybody's here, boss," said Harley. She was glassy-eyed from the drug, but otherwise, unless you count the mind control, still her usual self.

"I hear breathing," said Glen. "It's unmistakable." More loudly, "I don't know how anybody could breathe so loudly and think that they're doing a good job of hiding."

Being very talented at what he did, he closed his eyes for a moment and listened for Tabitha's breathing. She was under the bed. He followed his ears to the bed, then crouched down and said, "I found you. I'm surprised you can fit under this bed, if I'm to be perfectly honest with you."

"Haha, another fat joke," Tabitha said from under the bed.

"Get out from under there."

"No."

"You want me to drag you out?"

"I'd be surprised if you could, and I don't think it would turn out well for you."

He grabbed her arm and she bit him hard. "Ow!" He kept pulling through the pain, and she was out from under the bed. And everybody was out from their hiding spots because a matriarch was in distress.

She released his hand, which she had been biting, leaving deep tooth prints in it. Glen rubbed his hand and laughed low.

"I regret not having a wife I can go home and show this to."

"You need to watch your filthy fucking mouth!" said Frank-furt.

"You should have said that to your wife," said Glen, staring at Tabitha with obvious lust in his eyes, that Frankfurt punched him.

"It's going to have to get a whole lot more polite around here," said Andromedo, "because I don't want to see my best friend go to jail for murdering a police officer."

"Listen," said Glen. "I think it's common knowledge by now that I had sex with your wife."

"Actually, you didn't," said Frankfurt, relaxing a little bit.

"Oh, I most certainly did."

"No, you didn't," said Tabitha.

"Don't gaslight me. I'm the only gaslighter around here. I remember most everybody I've ever had sex with and Tabitha is on that list."

"I knocked you out and made you dream about having had sex with me. It was to keep on your good side."

"Yeah, buddy, she's done this to me too when she's not in the mood for actual sex," said Frankfurt.

"Let's solve this once and for all," said Glen, with a gift for prestidigitation, he stuck Tabitha in the neck with some drugs. "This is truth serum."

They were all shocked by what had just happened.

"Tabitha, did you have sex with me on multiple occasions?"

"No."

"Have you ever had sex with me?"

"No, only in your dreams."

He cursed. "How far have we gone, in that respect?"

"We kissed each other. Then I knocked you out and made you dream about having sex with me."

He looked at Frankfurt. "I guess you were right." He then hit Frankfurt in the neck with another syringe. "This one's mind control. I just need you to stop inflicting violence on me."

You really had to be very specific when it came to mind control, otherwise you could get the Evil Genie Effect. So Glen could have said, "Stop punching me," and then Frankfurt stop punching him, but begin kicking him. So he had to be careful about his phrasing.

He asked Tabitha, "Did you like kissing me?"

"Meh, fair to middling, I liked kissing Sergeant Marybeth better."

"Do you love me?"

"No."

"My marriage was broken up for nothing."

"You were the one who decided to live the kind of lifestyle where you blackmail women under the duress of their life, into giving you affection," said Tabitha. "I definitely wouldn't have stayed married to you under those circumstances."

He gave Tabitha another shot in the neck. "This one's mind control. I need you to take me to see my wife."

"Sir, you have no wife."

"My ex-wife."

"Okay."

"Hey stop that!" said Andromedo, who was still in his right mind, but Tabitha took off with Sergeant Glen to go see his wife.

"Stop right here," said Sergeant Glen, when they got out to the woods. Tabitha stopped there, landing, and getting off of her broom. Sergeant Glen got off of the broom, too, standing close to Tabitha. "I want to kiss you but I don't want you to be under mind control."

"That's your fault," said Tabitha. Perceiving a command, she kissed him passionately, but he broke away from her.

"I'm having trouble controlling myself right now. Let me ask you this. Do you love me?"

"You already asked me that and I already told you that I don't love you. Why? Do you need me to love you?"

He was silent for a moment. "It would be nice if somebody loved me." He shook his head. "Kiss me again, please."

So she kissed him again, and they kissed like a couple of teenagers first discovering kissing. He rubbed his nose against hers.

"Why are you so obsessed with me?" asked Tabitha, between kisses.

"Because it feels like my body is on fire when you're close to me."

She pushed him away. "If you are serious, take away the mind control."

Chapter 14

"Harley, we need you to follow them," said Andromedo, since Frankfurt was out of commission. "Frankfurt, I need you to snap out of it. I mind control you to stop being mind controlled, same with you Harley."

They snapped out of it and Kelly was very impressed.

"Hop on!" said Harley, back to her awesome self. She was very serious.

So these three plus sized (one in height, the other two in buffness, one in bustiness) adults piled onto Harley's stretch broom behind her, and they flew off in whatever direction Harley's witch's mind was leading her. She flew with purpose.

Glen had to think about that one. On one hand, he wanted them to keep kissing, on the other hand, he loved Tabitha. It wasn't logical nor was it good for him nor was it reciprocated, but he loved her. And he wanted her to love him too. She was right.

"You're right, you're right," he said. He reached into his fanny pack and took out another syringe.

"This one's usually meant for me," he said, and stuck her in the neck. Just as Harley, with Frankfurt, Andromedo, and Kelly on the back, flew into the scene to stop whatever was going on, arriving just as they saw Glen stick Tabitha in the neck with another syringe, and Andromedo yelled out, "I mind control you not to be mind-controlled!"

"You guys need to stop getting us involved in adventures on what was supposed to be our wedding day," said Kelly, fanning herself.

"I'm sorry pretty lady, pretty ladies," which was how women of their coven addressed each other.

"Sir!" said Andromedo, because he was in best of minds out there, "We have all witnessed you acting outside of the law, and I will make it one of my life's many missions to make sure you get fired."

Tabitha took a moment to feel sorry for Sergeant Glen, the guy who Sergeant Marybeth described as "special-minded." Frankfurt was special minded, but not like this.

"He was freeing me from the mind control," she said, now quite high due to all the drugs she'd been getting.

"That's nice Tabitha but he shouldn't have you on drugs in the first place, he is a cochino." Cochino means swine and was a popular word in their world for casual verbal abuse. It means the same thing in Spanish on our world. (There are many languages that sound like Spanish on their world.)

"I am not a cochino," said Glen. "How dare you?"

"How dare you, sir!"

Frankfurt sat next to Tabitha while Andromedo j'accused Sergeant Glen, and for his own good Frankfurt said, "Harley, we should get going before Andromedo gets into trouble."

Meanwhile, back at The Rich Harlot, Benny and Molly were taking a bubble bath. Although nobody had said anything to them about it yet, each likely were thinking, "Oh thank goodness, they're finally bathing," as they hadn't had a bath since they were back in Irrorria, days ago. This was the logic they used to take the bath. Molly had practically hopped over to it and said, "Look baby, there's a bath." And they took a bath in the fanciest hotel in all of Gargantua.

The bath was quite large and easily fit both of their skinny bodies in it, shaped in a large circle semisphere, and it was white as if bleached a few times that day, high quality ceramic. There were jets, and there was a bubble disaster where bubbles got everywhere.

Benny and Molly were beside themselves with happiness, and luckily covered up to the chest in bubbles, when everybody arrived and there was an awkward moment but Molly said, "We were really needing a bath!" and luckily due to Gargantuan hospitality which is quite hospitable, everybody had a good laugh, and they left them alone to the bath and hung out in a different part of the hotel suite.

Sergeant Glen was left alone after everyone flew off, and he remembered the real reason why he went to The Rich Harlot. That was to arrest Benny and Molly (he'd done his research and knew their names now). He'd gotten distracted with this love stuff with Tabitha. Why couldn't she love him the way he loved her? He meant to go to his wife, to demand that she tell her that they'd never had sex, but she was his ex-wife and he'd gotten distracted by being in love with Tabitha.

He could write epic poems about how much is sucked to be in love and for the other person not to love you back. He had written epic poems about that and was a very popular villain poet. He was particularly good at the villanelle. He wrote about multiple women because there were a few women out there whom he loved who didn't love him back. Tabitha was just one of them.

He shook his head and tried to get his mind back on track. He needed to go arrest Benny and Molly. They had tried to kill him; he definitely recognized them. Of course, being a villain, arrest wasn't the only thing he was going to do to them.

He started walking in the direction of the city. He had a wedding to ruin.

Chapter 15

"So are you disappointed not to be getting married today?" Harley asked Kelly, as they waited on Benny and Molly to rejoin them.

"A little bit but mostly just taken aback by today's events," said Kelly. "Tabitha, how long has this thing with that Sergeant Glen fellow, been going on?"

"It's a rare occurrence, happens once every few years," Tabitha said honestly.

"And you didn't tell me about it?"

"I didn't want you to think less of me."

"How could I ever think anything but nice thoughts about you?" said Kelly. "It's just you've got this handsome guy kissing you, and he's not Frankfurt, and there's a lot to process there."

"I'm not in love with the other guy," said Tabitha. "I'm not even in like with him."

"I mean, who hasn't kissed a guy to get out of execution, right?" said Kelly. Harley shrugged; it hadn't ever happened to her. Nobody ever tried to execute her, nor tried to kiss her to save her from it.

Harley was super-model pretty. Which was why guys minded their P's and Q's around her. And she was good about never doing things or being things that could get her arrested. It was far too easy to get killed in that time and place.

"I'm so glad you understand," Tabitha said.

"It's too bad Sven isn't a cop," said Harley all of a sudden. "Because he is an uncomplicated cutie pie. I'd let him arrest me."

The other women agreed that Sven was very cute. Though he looked just like Glen, he had never villainized them and therefore that added cuteness points to him. And they had all seen him nearly naked, nothing to complain about there. Sven himself had not yet been fully talked into becoming a police officer, but Glen was working on him. He'd say things like, "Come on, the police station needs a guy with a good heart like you." Whereas Sven didn't want to be a police officer and thought that being an exotic dancer was better, and he had to admit being a police officer would mean taking a pay cut. For what? Respectability in a society that sent him to a mamp once? He considered himself a freedom dancer, and was already gaining the respect of the other exotic dancers for being such a good exotic dancer.

"Ladies, I need to call an emergency coven meeting," said Kelly. Well, they were all there already, at least from this branch of the coven. They gathered round and held hands, the three of them. "Tabitha, be honest. Are you attracted to Sergeant Glen?"

"Ugh, no, maybe a little bit."

"That's okay, because we're going to nip that in the bud."

"Ha, thank you."

"BEGONE DEMON MAN

TAKE YOUR INTERESTS ELSEWHERE

LEAVE TABITHA ALONE."

"So this is supposed to help me not be attracted to Sergeant Glen, whom I only admit to the slightest amount of attraction to him."

"Yes, and better yet, not see him." Kelly was so serious about this. She wasn't about to have Tabitha's marriage jinxing her marriage with misfortune. They went through the magical rituals to make to ensure marital bliss between partners.

It was then that George and Eda showed up at the door. (Remember the half-baboon Irrorrian president and his wife/first lady?) "The wedding party moved here!" George said. "I thought you two were just going to be here, but, no, there's a whole witch's coven and everything. Fantastic!"

Eda said, "Who is the demon man?" looking at George suspiciously.

"Not him," Kelly said, earning a smile from Eda.

"So you're the cheater!" said George.

"No, no, I'm not a cheater," said Tabitha. "Stop trying to make everybody else like you. We all aren't just like you. You're a billionaire and I'm a housewife/serial smalltime entrepreneur, and it's okay for us to be different."

"So who's the demon man?"

"Nunya beeswax, that's who."

"Tabitha, is the president being weird again?" Frankfurt called from within another room of the hotel suite.

"Yes!" she called back. "Sir, just because I am your security guard and broomstick ride sharing taxi does not mean you can ask me personal questions and expect me not to be offended. I could quit as your security right now."

"Yeah, I guess that would be bad."

"It would be bad, especially considering that you've had assassination attempts on you recently."

"So you would just let me die for being offensive?"

"I just wouldn't work for you. It's not the same as letting you die."

"It kind of is."

"Sir, working for you, I've been bit several times, at odds with my good friend, and nearly hit with a kunai covered in poop."

Chapter 16

Languages on their world were very similar to languages on our world. In that there are a lot of them and they sound similar in various ways. Currently, the elite journalists Miranda and Jessica, were trying to get a hold of their Gargantuan language skills to navigate stalking the president. They weren't stalking the president in any way that was unconstitutional. They were just trying to get news. Which almost entirely covered their stalking, legally speaking.

"Ugh, nobody speaks Irrorrian here," said Miranda, tired of unproductive conversations with people who 1) she didn't understand and 2) didn't understand her.

"I've got an app that helps," said Jessica. "It's called Gargantuan for the Complete Nincompoop, which is admittedly a mouthful, but that's like how their language is."

"Can you read in Gargantuan?"

"I can."

"I need you to navigate my Broomr app."

"Okay."

"Yeah, I need you to book a flight to go see the President of Irrorria."

"I'll book a flight."

"Oh, look, someone's booked a flight," said Tabitha, happy to go back to work and avoid all the uncomfortable conversation everyone was engaging in over here at The Rich Harlot. "I will see you all later. I promise to turn off the app when it's time for your wedding."

"You better or I'll curse you," said Kelly, only half joking.

"Should I stay? I can stay."

"Go, and take everybody with you. You all can fly brooms, I know Frankfurt's secret in that he flies brooms. Go, take your friends, take Harley, we're going to kick out the President and his wife. Thank you for the hotel room."

"Gotcha, going, thank you for that, I wish you all the luck and will be there as soon as the wedding is even almost underway."

"I will let you know, pretty lady."

Tabitha flew off in the direction that the Broomr app was telling her to go, feeling thankful for the distraction. She felt sorry for Frankfurt, having such a wife as her. While it wasn't her fault that she was being mind-controlled, she still felt that if she had done things differently, this wouldn't be a problem. Thanks to the incantations, she was no longer attracted to Sergeant Glen, however that would affect their dynamic between each other.

It was early evening when she arrived at the Airport, where two confused looking Irrorrian women were waiting on her. One of them spoke into her cell phone, which translated her speech into Gargantuan. (The two languages were similar enough that they were mutually intelligible to people with really good ears for language, and everybody else got by using their cell phones this way.)

"Do you know where the president of Irrorria is?" the woman's cell phone asked her. She pulled out her own cell phone, opening the Gargantuan to Irrorrian app, and spoke into it.

"That depends. Are you trying to assassinate him?"

Because she wouldn't be a good security guard if she just brought the assassins to him, and she knew better than to think that just because these women were human and female, that they couldn't be assassins.

"No, we're news reporters," said the woman with the cell phone.

Tabitha, tired of her cell phone and all of its apps, decided to try her luck with Irrorrian. "You know, I can speak Irrorrian." Hoping that they wouldn't get offended, because some Irrorrians didn't like it when Gargantuans could speak Irrorrian.

"Oh, good," said Jessica. "I'm Jessica and this is Miranda, and we have a radio show where we follow around the president and try to see what news is happening around him."

"He's at a very fancy hotel right now," said Tabitha, having the most minimal of trouble keeping up but understanding most of what they were saying. "It costs a lot to get in there."

"Oh, money is no issue," said Jessica.

"We're exorbitantly rich," said Miranda, and, as if to prove it, she pulled out a higher than what was expected bill, and handed it to Tabitha, who promptly pocketed it.

"Well, then, to The Rich Harlot we go," said Tabitha.

"Really, he's at a hotel called The Rich Harlot?" said Miranda, giggling.

"I've got a wedding party there, too," said Tabitha. "Though I think that the bride and the groom could probably use some alone time. They've likely kicked everyone out already."

Kelly and Andromedo hadn't kicked everybody out yet, but they didn't have to, because their guests had the good sense to leave. The president and his wife had to be kicked out, but

Harley, Frankfurt, and Benny and Molly flew off to Frankfurt's home without any prompting.

Tabitha flew Jessica and Miranda from the airport, through the urban part of the city, past the rural areas, back into another urban area, and into The Rich Harlot. When she deposited them there, Jessica said, "Do you have time to stay with us, because we might still need transport?"

Tabitha said, "Is this time paid for?"

Miranda said, "Absolutely," and gave her some more money for her trouble. "So do you know where the president is at?"

"Yes, I do."

She waited on them to get checked into the hotel, then led them to the president's room. They stood aside for her to knock on the door.

"Mr. President? It's me, Tabitha. The news requested that I bring them to see you."

The president opened the door, then scowled at Miranda and Jessica.

"You two!"

And he shut the door again. "Tabitha, you're fired."

"I didn't quite hear that sir," said Tabitha, who hadn't quite heard him. He opened the door again.

"You're fired."

"But why, sir?" she asked. "I would think you would want the news to know about the insurgency movement in your country."

"Why would I want them to know about that?"

"Insurgency movement?" repeated Miranda. "What's all that about?"

"They've been trying to assassinate him for the past day," said Tabitha. "I've taken on the role of security guard to keep him safe, and it seems as though the trouble has passed."

"Who's been trying to assassinate him?"

George physically grabbed Tabitha and pulled her into the room, shutting the door after her.

"Tabitha, you probably aren't used to this level of responsibility," said George, redder in the face than usual, "but you possess what are known as 'state secrets.' Because you possess these secrets, the one thing you must make sure not to do, is tell anybody about them."

"I've told quite a few people since picking you up this morning about this," said Tabitha. "We talked to your mother and your wife about it. I told Kelly and Andromedo, and of course Frankfurt and Harley know about it. And if you're going to make all of us disappear, disappear us to someplace nice, okay?"

"I'm not disappearing any of you," said George. "That's saved for a different kind of political enemy."

"Who's disappearing honey?" said Eda, walking into the foyer.

"Nobody's disappearing!" huffed George.

"Come on, let me work with these nice ladies to figure out some socially acceptable version of the news!" said Tabitha. "I can still protect you while working for the news."

"If they think that Edington has turned on me, it'll cause mass chaos and panic."

"So do you have a version of the news that you want me to report back to these women?"

"Yes. Everything is fine. Don't worry. The assassination attempts have been stopped."

"Okay, that sounds good," said Tabitha. "Am I still fired?"

George sighed. "Not fired, per se, but I don't know if I'll have continued need for your service now that the assassination attempts have stopped. However, thank you for your service to the Irrorrian government."

"Ew," said Tabitha. "I never thought about it that way."

She stepped outside of the president's suite and addressed Miranda and Jessica.

"The president says that everything is fine. The assassination attempts have been thwarted. And there's nothing further to report."

Jessica and Miranda looked at each other, then at this pleasantly plump and from the looks of it, naïve witch, and they smiled.

"What are those bite marks on you?" asked Miranda, with a journalist's eye for details.

"That happened during an earlier trip, when someone on drugs attacked me," said Tabitha, careful to leave out that Edington the Butler was the one who did it.

"You must have a very exciting job!" breathed Jessica, almost as though she wished that her job involved getting bitten by druggies.

"Meh, it can get that way sometimes," said Tabitha. "Most the time it's just the same old same old."

"I've lately been considering a career change to hospitality," said Jessica, with a nod from Miranda. "Less stress."

"Less money," said Tabitha astutely.

"Listen," said Miranda, smarter than she usually was because she hadn't had any margaritas in a small while, "why don't you come back to the hotel room with us and tell us all about life as a Gargantuan. It's a complete mystery to us Irrorrians."

"This is a paying gig?" Tabitha said wisely. She smiled a little bit at the growing looks of respect on her ride sharers' faces, knowing that they thought she must be some country bumpkin, and also that they were easy with their money.

"Absolutely," said Miranda, giving Tabitha some more money.

By this time tomorrow, Tabitha would definitely be able to pay back her late rent. She followed them into their hotel room.

"You two aren't weirdos, by the way?" she asked, stepping over the threshold. "Because my husband really wouldn't want me going into the hotel room of a couple of weirdos, no offense."

"Not that kind of weirdo that you need to fear in hotels," said Jessica. "Cat collecting weirdos, yes. Assaulting people in hotels weirdos, no."

"Oh, I like cat collectors," said Tabitha. She had a familiar back at home who was a black cat named Jackie. Not much up to this point has been written about Jackie, but she has an active and adventurous life as a witch's familiar and semi-wild cat.

"So, Tabitha, tell us about yourself," said Jessica, holding up a recorder.

Tabitha cleared her throat and then realized that she had nothing to say. What if they misreported everything she said and made her look bad? Frankfurt was already putting up with too much from her, by her own standards, to have to deal with her on the news making them look bad.

"Jessica, Jessica, you're doing this wrong," said Miranda. She went to the mini-bar and procured a margarita in a bottle. "Have a margarita," she told Tabitha. Tabitha held up a hand.

"Oh, I couldn't, I'm working tonight."

"We'll pay for you to stay as long as you need," said Miranda. "Matter of fact, this place has a real bar. What are we messing about with a mini-bar for? Let's go find the real bar!"

Sighing, Tabitha followed them out of the room and into the real bar. George and Eda were there.

"Where's your butler?" asked Marissa boisterously in Irrorrian.

"He's indisposed," said George, moving a seat over when she sat next to him. "How are you doing, Tabitha?"

"Bone-tired, sir."

"You've had quite an eventful day, haven't you?"

"Super-eventful, sir."

"It's about to get more eventful!" said Jessica.

"I had no idea you could speak Irrorrian," said George.

"Yeah, I'm alright at it."

"No, you sound super-good. Almost can't tell your Gargantuan, with that accent."

Tabitha smiled tiredly. "These are closely related languages." She sighed. "I have to call my husband." She dialed him on the phone.

Frankfurt sounded as though he was in a busy household. Their household. "Hello?" he asked, shushing the kids around him.

"Hi sweetheart, I'm back at The Rich Harlot."

"Why are you there? We've done all the business we could there."

"I got another couple of ride sharing guests who wanted to go there."

"Not the police officer, eh?"

"ARBOR no, and I am so sorry about that."

"You should apologize, for being so sexy."

"I'm sorry, honey."

"I'm kidding. Enjoy your stay. I've got the kids; they're fine." A beat. "When will you be home?"

"These couple of ride sharers invited me for money to the bar."

"Sounds sketchy."

"They're journalists."

"I stand by what I said."

"They're women journalists."

"I'm only slightly less apprehensive hearing that."

"Really, if you must know, I was planning on working all night so that the bill is definitely paid by tomorrow."

"Ugh, I hate having bills," Frankfurt moaned.

"It's just one night," said Tabitha. "I'm almost there, monetarily speaking."

"Less talky, more drinky," Miranda said beside her.

"That gibberish sounds like it was directed at you," said Frankfurt.

"It was. These journalists want to get me drunk. They only speak Irrorrian."

"Well, then, don't give away any family secrets."

"Okay, dear." And she got off the phone with him. George scooted next to her.

"Tell me, how did you hook up with these losers?" he asked in Gargantuan, nodding at Jessica and Miranda.

"Same way as with you, through the app," said Tabitha. She really was super-tired. If homelessness wasn't the looming other alternative, she would be at home, relaxing with her family. Or cleaning dishes or something. Maybe she would have called a day off and gone covening with her lady friends. It had been a long time since they'd had a proper coven meeting, not an emergency one sprouted from her personal problems.

"They're tabloid journalists," George continued. "They stole my DNA before!"

"No, dear, I gave them your DNA," Eda said.

"It wasn't yours to give," huffed George. "It was theft by receiving."

Tabitha was mildly amused. "What did they want with your DNA?"

"It's a long story but my butler Edington is the father of some children who look as though they could be mine," grumbled George, "to an untrained, ignorant specist eye."

"How many kids do you have that aren't mine?" Eda asked, for the second time that night.

"I don't know, minus three."

"Stop talking to these politicians," Miranda said, already into her first margarita. "Talk to us. What's new in Gargantua?"

"Well, math was decriminalized," said Tabitha, looking at the drink they set before her, with exhaustion. "I don't really know the news around here, too much, because I'm too busy working and taking care of my family to get really into it." She took a sip of her margarita.

Chapter 17

"Drink drink drink!" Miranda and Jessica were chanting at Tabitha. Though she rarely ever drank, somehow they had talked her into letting them turn her upside down so she could drink directly from a beer keg, as if that was sanitary. (If she was sober, she'd have never done this.) She drank, and they set her right side up again.

"So," said Jessica, excited to have gotten this enigmatic foreigner drunk, "tell us all about yourself."

"It starts off as a once upon a time," warned Tabitha. They nodded to keep her talking. "Once upon a time, there were royals who lived in this land. The people didn't like them, so they killed them all, as well as their children. Only a few lucky ones escaped, and their kids were sent off to live as peasants."

"Really?" said Jessica. "I've never heard about that."

"The royal purge or the survivors?"

"Neither! There was news about how Gargantua was a democracy now, but there was never any reporting of a purge."

"Yeah, well, you know, the news omits what they don't want you to know."

"From what I heard," slurred Miranda, who was now very drunk, "royals and other such were still very much alive and well, and simply propagate that lie so that people will feel sorry for them. As they say, stay vigilant, student of history."

"No, they killed the shit out of them," said Tabitha resolutely.

"So you say that their kids were raised as peasants," said Jessica, who was more sober and therefore able to pick up on more details than Miranda, which was their usual dynamic.

"Yes," said Tabitha. She paused for a moment. "There's a lot worse things out there than getting raised as a peasant. Like death, for example."

"Whatever became of these royal peasants?" asked Jessica.

"Meh, they grew up to be working class adults, got jobs, that kind of thing," said Tabitha. "And there's a Gargantuan prince scammer out there who claims to be a prince and could escape for Whalery if someone would just pay the way for him."

That was Tabitha's brother Larry, unbeknownst to her. He wasn't a scammer; he was a beggar. But the thing he was begging for, that was legit. He really did want to escape to Whalery, and no jobs he was able to get, were able to pay for that privilege.

"It makes sense these royals would grow up to be scammers," said Miranda.

"That's only one of them. The rest blend in with regular society as to not get killed."

Tabitha was feeling agitated; this conversation was not going the way she would have hoped. It was then when she saw a trio of familiar faces, The Bajingo Band, Eric, Billy Bob, and Bubba.

"Tabitha, it's you!" said Eric, the one to recognize her because the other two slept through their ride home. "How are you doing?"

"So tired, brothers," she said. "I have a wedding to go to in just a few hours, and I don't know how I'm going to make it."

"Hey!" said Miranda, possessive. "Get your own ride sharing

taxi!"

"What did she just say?" said Bubba to Billy Bob, who shrugged.

"I think she thinks that you're cute," Billy Bob said to Bubba.

Miranda did not understand enough Gargantuan to protest this. Billy Bob was pulling Bubba's leg. Bubba was fashionably ugly; nobody ever called him cute. Some women found him attractive anyway, and that was because they were attracted to unattractive. Different strokes for different folks, you know.

"Did you guys need a ride anywhere?" Tabitha asked irresponsibly, hiccupping. Normally she never drank (at least not much) so she didn't have that necessary filter to tell when she'd been drinking too much to navigate a broomstick.

"Not now, but in ten minutes, we'll be needing a ride to Gargantuan station to do a concert."

"Ek, people are still coming out to see music?"

"How is it that someone who hates the night as much as you do, works the night shift?"

"I don't hate the night. I just kind of prefer to be sleeping around this hour."

"Did you just agree to do another ride share?" Jessica asked Tabitha in Irrorrian.

"Yes."

"But you're drunk," she said.

"It's a broomstick," slurred Tabitha. "What's the worst that can happen?"

"Be careful!" Eric the bajingo star was yelling at Tabitha as she just barely missed a tree. "I thought you were more responsible than this!"

"I am very responsible!" Tabitha said, contradicting herself with her actions. She turned to face him. "I don't know why you would question my responsibility levels."

"Because you're about to hit another tree, keep your eyes ahead of you!"

She narrowly missed the tree and he kept talking.

"I thought I remembered you saying that you don't drink."

"I don't normally, but they were paying for me to."

"Why were they paying for you to drink?"

"Because they're news women and thought that I had some interesting stories to tell, which I don't."

"I'm sure you do, everybody's got a story in them," said Eric.

"None for the news," said Tabitha. A beat. "You lot still worship the devil?"

Eric shrugged, which Tabitha felt as a shift in weight on the broom. "No, that got old. Attracts a weird crowd, you know."

"So are you ARBORists now, or did you jump on the bandwagon and become unreligious like me?"

"Don't try to slap a label on us, love."

"Hey, at least I don't have to worry about you all trying to cannibalize me now."

"Ha ha ha ha ha. That joke never gets old."

She deposited them at the concert, and then decided that it was time to go home, finally. The rain had finally stopped and the crickets were out making a lot of noise, and she flew away from the crowded stadium taking a moment to appreciate how beautiful everything looked. It seemed like every star in space was in the sky at that moment.

She was halfway home, taking about half an hour, when her phone beeped again.

"Son of a..." and she cursed for a while there. She looked, and realized, "Hey, there are other ride sharers out there. I don't need to turn back."

So she kept going. Her eyes were having trouble staying open. She tried to fly through the exhaustion, but ended up falling, falling, falling, until she hit the ground, which was luckily covered in pine straw.

Chapter 18

Sergeant Glen was still walking, still considering how he was going to ruin this wedding if he got to it in time, when he came across Tabitha, asleep on the ground. She was bleeding lightly from her forehead.

In every villain's life, there comes sometimes a time when he can decide to keep being a jerk, or do something nice. He poked Tabitha with his shoe a few times.

"Tabitha. Tabitha!"

"What!"

"You're asleep in the middle of the woods. You have to get up, or you'll get eaten by a bear."

Though frankly, he thought, he felt sorry for any bear that would try to eat her. Probably she would eat the bear.

"Shut up and go away," she said.

He thought about it. But how was he going to earn her love if he abandoned her in the middle of a forest at night? Then he thought, how was he going to earn her love at all? She was already in love, with her fat, stupid husband.

Selflessly, he picked her up. "Wow, you're heavy."

"No more fat jokes."

"It wasn't a joke, it was a statement of fact."

"Size is relative."

"I'm not calling you fat. I'm calling you heavy. There is a difference."

He put her on his back, and she wrapped her arms around him, and he told himself this is what it felt like to be loved.

"Did you know that you are harboring three fugitives that tried to kill me?"

"I know nothing."

"I've seen you with three people today that tried to kill me."

"Have you ever wondered maybe why you have so many attempts at your life?"

"No."

"Could you take a moment to think about it?"

He considered dropping her, but instead took a moment to think about why people were so keen on killing him.

"I would say that I can't help what I do for a living," said Glen, who was not only a police sergeant, but also a spy and a psychological operative for the government, "but I could. The thing is, this pays well and I'm good at it. Is that such a bad thing?"

"You drive people crazy."

"You were barely alive when the royals were about," said Glen. "I know you were a little kid back then, but they were not doing a good job of things."

"So your lot drove them crazy and killed them," said Tabitha bitterly. "And the mathematicians."

"You really have no idea the extent of my job," said Glen, "but sometimes it involves me being the hero."

"I bet you really like that."

"It's slightly more appreciated than being a villain."

"Tell me, what was the last heroic thing that you've done?"

"Other than picking you up here when I could have much more

easily left you to be eaten by bears?"

"You think you're so funny."

"I liberated a mamp."

"What, no!"

"Yasss."

"I was supposed to liberate that mamp."

"I suppose you're jealous of me, now."

"A little bit."

"ARBOR, your breath smells so alcoholic right now."

Frankfurt was asleep on his love seat, waiting on Tabitha. The wedding would take place in the morning, and he really hoped she wouldn't miss it. Both Kelly and Andromedo were at their wedding, and he didn't want to attend their wedding alone.

"Can you fly now?"

"I'm sure I can."

"Correction: can you fly without killing the both of us?"

"I can try."

"That's good, because it turns out I'm not the muscular hulk I thought I was. You are so heavy!"

"I can fly alone," she said, and he set her down.

"Do you think you could take me to go see my ex-wife?" he asked plaintively.

"Last time you wanted me to take you to your wife, you had me land in the middle of the forest and kiss you, which, now that I'm not under mind control, ew."

"You've kissed me before not under mind control."

"Yes, but under duress."

They walked, side by side.

"Are you even attracted to me?"

"No."

"I could have sworn that you were attracted to me."

"I was a little bit, but my coven cured me of it. Love and attraction are two different things. I'm in love with Frankfurt."

"Witches," he muttered underneath his breath. "What do you see in Frankfurt, anyway?"

"He's my soul mate. He's been there for me my entire life. If he wants a kiss, he just kisses me."

Glen stopped and kissed her on the mouth, and she punched him in the gut. Hard.

"Ow, what was that for?"

"Duh, I'm not in love with you. I'm not attracted to you."

"Then why did you kiss me all those times in the first place?"

"Because I appreciate being alive. Dude, you don't know women at all."

"Maybe I don't."

Chapter 19

Tabitha ended up flying Sergeant Glen mostly to his ex-wife, dropping him off early because she didn't want to see her. She was staying at their old house. Walking with as much pride as he could muster, he went and rang the doorbell.

Quinn, his wife, opened the door for a moment to see who it was, and then when she saw Glen out there waiting on her, she closed the door, but he stuck his foot in the door jam.

"I need to talk to you."

"That's funny, because I need to not talk to you."

"I was an idiot."

"That's a statement of fact if I've ever heard one."

"I never had sex with Tabitha."

"Pfft."

"No, she put me under a spell to think that I had sex with her."

"Not my problem."

"The whole time, I was distracted by other women, when I should have been distracted by you."

"We agree on this. Now go!"

He thought about leaving but still wasn't ready to go. "Will you ever forgive me?"

"Of course. I've already forgiven you. I just don't want to be married to you."

"Story of my life," he muttered.

Tabitha arrived at home, more than bone tired, more than dead tired, and found Frankfurt on the loveseat, asleep. She snuggled up next to him, and before she could even get very comfortable, was asleep as well.

Chapter 20

The day of Kelly and Andromedo's wedding started out with a bright sunrise, which Tabitha totally missed because she was asleep and if she wasn't asleep, would have been hung-over. Tabitha woke up to the sound of the phone ringing. She was beginning to hate her phone.

"Hello?" she croaked, squeezing past Frankfurt to get off of the loveseat to grab her phone.

"Don't tell me you forgot about my wedding, pretty lady," said Kelly, sounding effervescent.

"No, I haven't. What time is that?"

"It's in two hours."

"What? ARBOR time flies."

"Are you going to be there?"

"Of course!"

Getting off the phone, she woke up Frankfurt, saying, "It's time to wake up. The wedding is in two hours."

She and Frankfurt woke up, and then they woke up the kids, who were sleeping in because it was a Saturday. Tom and Jon greatly protested waking up early on a Saturday.

"Mom, this is supposed to be our sleeping in day," moaned Tom.

"Did you know that most teenagers don't get enough sleep?" inquired Jon.

"There's no time for argument. Your aunt and uncle Kelly and Andromedo are getting married today."

"I thought that was yesterday," said Tom.

"No, it's today."

"We're going to a wedding?"

"Yes!"

The two hustled up to find their nicest suits. Next it was time to wake up Marissa. Only Marissa wasn't in her bed. Instead some boy named Wilbert was there.

"Tabitha, there's a boy in Marissa's bed!" yelled Frankfurt from across the house.

"Dad, it's me," said Wilbert. "I told Mom I always wanted to be a boy, so she changed me into one using magic." He looked closely at his new son and recognized Marissa's features.

Tabitha came into the room and remembered that Wilbert was Marissa, just in boy form.

"Oh, that's right. I magicked Marissa into a boy, yesterday. Meet Wilbert."

Frankfurt said, "You can't just make unilateral parenting decisions like that. You should have at least told me about it first, or afterwards, instead of letting me discover this way."

"Am I a handsome boy?" asked Wilbert.

"Very handsome," both parents said, and Frankfurt added, "So what are you going to wear to the wedding?"

It was at this point Wilbert panicked, because he didn't have any male dress clothes.

"Pick out your favorite dress," Tabitha commanded.

"But Mom, I don't want to go back to being a girl," said Wilbert.

"That's not what I'm doing. Just pick a dress."

Wilbert sullenly picked a dress out of his closet, and with a wave of her trusty wand, the dress turned into a suit.

"Aw, Mom, you're the best!"

Next it was time to dress up and feed Tobey and Penelope. Frankfurt complained as she did so.

"You know, this messes up our sons to daughters ratio. What if our kids are in a movie together? They'll fail the Bechtel test, because there won't be enough women in it to have a conversation about something other than men."

"What's the Bechtel test?" asked Tabitha, who hadn't been going to night classes because she'd already completed her witch's apprenticeship years ago.

"Never you mind, we're barely going to make it to the wedding in time, at this rate."

Tabitha strapped baby Penelope to her front with a stretchy kangaroo pouch kind of outfit, and Tobey hung onto her leg. So she put him in the stretchy pouch as well, and soon both very well dressed toddlers were asleep on their mother's chest.

"Is everybody ready to go?" she asked.

"Yes!"

"Yes, let's go!"

So she and Frankfurt loaded up on their brooms, Frankfurt wearing a wig just in case because only women were supposed to fly brooms (and frankly he was too afraid to have Tabitha turn him into a woman for any period of time), and their older children loaded up behind them, Tom and Jon behind Tabitha and Wilbert behind Frankfurt. Benny and Molly stayed home, since they didn't really know Andromedo and Kelly that well, and to babysit Toby and Penelope, the youngest two.

It was a gloriously beautiful day. Tabitha and Frankfurt made sure to wear their sunglasses so that they wouldn't get the sun in their eyes. About halfway there, Tabitha realized she didn't know exactly where their wedding was, so she called up Kelly, who told her to meet them at The Rich Harlot.

"We're doing the wedding here," said Kelly. "They have a chapel and everything."

So they flew to The Rich Harlot, and went to Kelly and Andromedo's room.

"Where's Benny and Molly?" Andromedo asked.

"They're back at home."

"They could have come to the wedding, we wouldn't have minded."

"The broomsticks were already pretty full."

"Did you dress up as a woman to fly your kids around?"

"I like your suit."

Kelly's phone rang. It was her mom.

"Yes, Mom, we're getting married at The Rich Harlot's chapel." There were some unintelligible sounds on the other end of the phone. "No, Mom, it's not bad luck to get married at a chapel at a place called The Rich Harlot. You should see their chapel. It's beautiful." Another few moments of talk on the other end. "Can you get a refund? No? Damn!"

After getting off of the phone with her mother, Kelly said, "We're going to have to go to The First Temple of ARBOR, because Mom already paid for us to get married there."

"They don't have a refund policy?" asked Andromedo.

"No."

Andromedo had some choice words for temples without refund policies. There was a knock at the door, and there was Harley and her trusty broomstick.

"Hi, I heard there's a wedding here today?"

"We were wrong," sighed Andromedo. "It's at the First Temple of ARBOR, because they don't have a refund policy."

"That's okay!" said Harley, who was at the core of her nature, a very cheerful witch. She looked over at Kelly, who was wearing a nice dress that wasn't her wedding dress. "Wow woman, you look hot."

"Thank you, pretty lady," said Kelly.

"When are you getting into your wedding dress?"

"Soon."

It was decided that the men (including the boys), should go first, and that the women should follow, so that Andromedo wouldn't see Kelly in her wedding dress. A few more ride sharers had to be called in, because people were multiplying quickly. Finally they all arrived at The First Temple/Power Station of ARBOR, which looked completely different in the blue sky than it looked in a storm.

Tabitha and Harley waited on Kelly who got into her dress, which was frothy, white, curve hugging masterpiece of a wedding gown. When she emerged, both Tabitha and Harley burst into tears.

"What is wrong with you two?"

"It's just that you look so beautiful!" Harley said, Tabitha nodding.

"Let us be the crybabies that we are!" Tabitha admonished, leading the three of them into a group hug. "We're so overwhelmed with happiness for you that it's leaking out of our eyes."

"Weirdos."

Tabitha walked out to check on Frankfurt, walking in on Andromedo, in a fine-looking white suit, panicking.

"I've forgotten the rings."

"What? How could you forget the rings? It's one of the most important objects in the ceremony?"

"Don't add to the trouble."

Tabitha took Andromedo back to get the rings. It was back at their house, not at The Rich Harlot.

"Thank you, Tabitha, this means the world to me," Andromedo said.

"No problem, you two need the rings, we'll get the rings."

Glen stood there with his brother Sven, ringing the door of his ex-wife. Looking like a Rurulian model, with very long blond hair in a triangular cut, Quinn rubbed her eyes and opened the door, and then she said, "There are two of you."

"Nice to meet you," said Sven, holding out a hand to shake with her. Bemused, she shook his hand. "I didn't know you married a Rurulian woman."

"I hope you don't have anything against the Rurulians," she said crossly.

"Not at all," said Sven. "I hear it is a lovely country. Now, if you were from Irrorria, I might have to do some soul searching to accept you."

"Whatchoo got against Irrorria?" she said, still cross.

"They interned me there for years with barely enough food to survive and made me do slave labor, and I saw so many people die," said Sven, struggling to keep a pleasant facial expression.

"Is this the mathematician?" she asked Glen.

"He's an exotic dancer now."

"Math is decriminalized now," said Sven, with dignity.

"It might be, but that doesn't mean I have to like you. Which brings me to my second point, which is, what are you two doing here?"

Glen said, "I just thought it would be nice to introduce you to my brother. You always said it was a shame you couldn't meet more of my family."

"That was when we were married. We're not married now. I don't even like you now. We're not friends. We're nothing."

"We're more than nothing," said Glen. "We're ex-spouses. That has to count for something."

Somehow they ended up inside of Quinn's house, more because she was tired of letting out the air conditioning than really wanting them in her house, and the news was happening on the TV.

"There has been an unusual level of zombie activity around The First Temple/Power Station of ARBOR..." said the newscaster, his very pretty co-newscaster raising her eyebrows at this phenomenon. "What do you think is causing this?"

"Obviously," said the other newscaster, "ARBOR is upset because there's been a downtick in human sacrifice since it was made illegal, so he's punishing us with more zombies."

"I heard that ARBOR didn't want anymore human sacrifice," said the other newscaster, which earned him getting slapped by his coworker. "Ow, what was that for?"

"ARBOR's favor," she said.

Quinn turned off the TV, with a loud sigh.

"Did you hear that there's a zombie uprising near the First Temple/Power Station of ARBOR?" Jessica asked Miranda, who was barely awake and still hung over from the night before.

"No."

"Well, there is one, so get up and get your news stuff together, because we're going to the First Temple/Power Station of ARBOR."

Miranda sighed loudly. "Following and reporting the news is exhausting. Maybe we should consider retiring to careers in hospitality."

"I get what you're saying, and we're just going to put a pin in it and stick it up here with all the other things you say that we put a pin in..."

"That just means that we'll never talk about it again."

"No, I mean, I could see myself getting into hospitality, but right now there's news to be reported." She got out her spritz bottle of water that she kept for occasions like this, and spritzed Miranda in the face.

"Hey, stop that."

"You up?"

"I'm up, don't do that anymore. You know I can't stand it when you spritz me in the face."

The two gathered together their work stuff for the news, and caught the first ride share to The First Temple/Power Station of ARBOR.

Chapter 21

"Mr. President, what are you doing here?" asked Kelly, who was waiting on Tabitha and Andromedo, and just saw the president at the power station.

"I thought you'd invited us to your wedding," he said, looking confused. His wife smiled apologetically at Kelly. "Also, I'm staying here in case there are any more attempts on my life, Tabitha can sort them out. Speaking of, where is she?"

"She's with Andromedo, getting our rings for the wedding," Kelly said. "Make yourself at home, she'll be back soon."

Kelly's parents, Sally and Reed, were nearby her, weeping happily over their baby girl's soon-to-be-matrimony. And then Sally realized that her daughter was talking to the president of Irrorria.

"Honey," she said to Kelly, "would you care to introduce us to your friend?"

Kelly sighed, not in the mood to explain to her mother that the president of Irrorria was not and never would be her friend.

"Mom, Dad, this is the president of Irrorria, George Franklington, and Eda Franklington, his wife, and these are my parents, Sally and Reed."

It turned out that Eda used to be a famous actress, so Sally was kind of starstruck, because she'd watched these two on television religiously before they got into politics. Reed was politely less impressed than his wife. Reed was a difficult guy to impress. You really had to change the world, in a way that Reed approved of, before he'd even consider being impressed by you.

"Nice to meet you two," he said, wondering in his great dolphin's brain, why on Earth were the president of another country and his famous, glamorous wife, at his daughter's wedding. Nobody in their friend group hung out in those kinds of circles. Eventually he deduced that this must be through Tabitha or Harley's ride sharing services, that they were acquainted. Which was a correct deduction.

"I loved you in The Child Genius," Sally told George, which was a show he'd acted in as a child, and the beginning of his great source of wealth.

"Thank you, I loved me in that, too," said George.

Andromedo got his rings from his bedroom, hopped back on the broomstick with Tabitha, and the two of them raced back to the temple/power station. They were almost there, and too focused to notice the zombies nearby that were clearly recognizable due to their stiff zombie gaits.

"Thank you so much, Tabitha," said Andromedo.

"No problem," she said. "I'm honored to help."

"You know, Kelly really likes you."

"I really like her too."

"She knows that we used to go out."

"Yeah, I shouldn't have lied all those times that she asked me about it, I don't know what's wrong with me."

"She's not bothered by it. We were teenagers."

"That's a big relief to me."

"She is bothered that you feel like you had to lie about it, though. She'd like to think that you two were closer than that and you could have really compared notes there or something."

"Oh, damn."

"It's not that big of a deal. I'm just trying to facilitate the friendship here, because I know your friendship makes her happy most of the time anyway, and I like when she's happy."

"Definitely. I'm really sorry about lying about it."

They arrived at the station at the same time as Miranda and Jessica, who was with Harley, who seemed most apologetic.

"Guys, there are zombies nearby."

Zombies on their world were not the zombie apocalypses of our world. But it still raised concern.

"Zombies? I haven't heard of any zombies since that math camp was torched," said Tabitha.

"Apparently they're coming from all around to talk to AR-BOR."

"Oh, see, and we're in the First Temple/Power Station of ARBOR, so here's where they would go," said Andromedo. He made a beeline to go see Kelly.

Tabitha stayed to talk to Harley, while Jessica and Miranda set up for their radio news bit.

"How do you think this is going to affect the wedding?" Tabitha asked Harley.

"It could be positive if Kelly, like me, thinks that zombies are romantic at weddings," Harley mused.

"What if one of them tries to eat our brains?"

"Oh, that's a stereotype. It's so rare that they try to do that."

"Okay..."

"Last I heard about a zombie eating somebody's brain, it was at that teacher's summit, one of the teachers died and became a zombie and ate that principal's brain. They just get a lot of bad press. Every time someone does something bad that's a zombie, it's in the news. It would make you think a massive gathering of them is dangerous, but not one of those zombies yet have eaten anybody's brains."

"Oh, well, that's a relief. I was thinking that maybe I was supposed to get out a weapon, and then I remembered that I have my wand and my broom, so it's like I'm already armed."

"You don't have to worry about it," said Harley. "I just think it's so romantic that zombies showed up for their wedding. That's true luck."

"Dubious luck at best," said Tabitha. "We all know that they're meant for each other. I've already let them know that I'll personally shun the both of them if they get divorced."

"That's a little extreme."

"That's how much I'm rooting for their marriage."

"So if I get married to the wrong guy and then get divorced, will you shun me?"

"Oh, no, that's different. These two are meant to be together. That's why I'm socially pressuring them to stay together."

"Only you, Tabitha," said Harley.

"Only me what?"

"Only you would think that's a good idea. What if they feel so pressured that they crack under the pressure and then get divorced?

"Then begins the shunning."

"Stop that!"

"Everybody needs at least one socially conservative friend to keep their marriage good."

"I don't know if I would describe you as socially conservative."

"When it comes to marriage between soul mates, I am. Now,

marriage between people who are obviously better off apart, then they can get divorced, but marriage between two people who are obviously meant for each other, needs society reinforcing that they are meant for each other so they don't go messing it up."

"You're a philosopher."

"Not so much."

Frankfurt went to find Andromedo who had gone to find Kelly, and he found the two of them in a corner of temple, completely abandoning their superstition about seeing one's bride in her dress before the wedding, by kissing each other.

"Oh, I'm sorry, I'll leave you two be," said Frankfurt, backing away. Andromedo waved a hand dismissively.

"Don't worry about it, we've just agreed to go on with the wedding, because it's not like something like a potential zombie apocalypse could stop it."

"I've heard these zombies are chill," said Frankfurt. "They haven't eaten anybody's brains yet."

"I think we should have machetes just in case one or all of them decide to start eating brains," said Andromedo.

"I'm a witch, so I'll be okay," said Kelly. "I don't know about you two."

"I'm learning witchery," said Frankfurt.

"Bro, so am I," said Andromedo.

"Most of it's been flying, though," said Frankfurt.

"Hey, until those zombies grow wings, that's legitimate," said Andromedo.

"Unless he gets arrested by the police," mentioned Kelly.

"I flew a police officer around, thank you very much, and she discovered I was a guy and still didn't arrest me," elaborated Frankfurt.

"That's nice," Kelly said distracted.

The preacher came over and told them that the wedding had been postponed, because the zombies were demanding to see ARBOR.

"I got this," said Tabitha, and dialed ARBOR on the phone. "ARBOR, we need you, there's a zombie uprising and my best friends here are trying to get married."

"I got this," said ARBOR, and suddenly appeared next to her in all of his corpulent glory. "I've heard that I'm needed?"

"How did you do that?" said the preacher, who was flabber-gasted.

"He's my meat guy," said Tabitha. "He's super-magic, his name is ARBOR, and none of us witches can compete with this guy, which is totally aggravating, no offense ARBOR."

The preacher and ARBOR went to address the zombies. The zombies were less discriminating than the usual ARBORists, and they seemed to accept this ARBOR just fine. Especially because one of the first things he did was conjure up a bunch of humanely magicked brains for them.

"Okay, so, I really think it's time now we got married," said Andromedo with as much patience and good humor as he could.

"I agree," said Kelly. "Forget these zombies. I could elope with you this moment if you wanted."

"Did somebody say that these two are getting married?" said ARBOR, magically back from his humane brain feeding miracle.

"Yes, can you marry them? They need to be married, like, yesterday," said Tabitha, who also couldn't wait for her best friends to be wedded in holy matrimony.

"Wedded by ARBOR himself," said Kelly smiling big. "Sounds good to me."

"Music!" said ARBOR, and the organist began playing an

upbeat "Here Comes The Bride," with some jazzy components to it, "Places!" And everybody magically found themselves in place.

"We are gathered here today," said ARBOR, "Because these two wonderful humans want to be together. Does anybody object to them being together?"

It was just at that time that Sergeant Glen arrived, apparently exhausted from having run there. "I object! If I'm not happy, why should they be happy?"

"Get the fuck out of here!" shouted various members of the congregation, and ARBOR, feeling sorry for the guy, magicked him back to his best friend/roommate Officer Bryant's apartment, in front of the TV, where his favorite movie was playing.

"This is nice," said Sergeant Glen, nestling up to a cat that was magically not there five minutes ago, "I can take a small vacation from being a villain now and watch this movie and maybe take a nap."

Back at the wedding, ARBOR said, "Can I have the rings, please?"

Andromedo gave him the rings. "I bless these rings that so long as you should have them, your marriage will be strong."

"Come on, ARBOR, what if they lose them?" said Tabitha.

"And that your marriage will be strong even if you lose the rings," he said for Tabitha's benefit. He gave a ring to Andromedo, and a ring to Kelly. Andromedo got the woman's ring and Kelly, the man's. "Place these on each other's fingers so that you two may always be together, even at the End of Time."

They placed the rings on each other's appropriate fingers.

"I now pronounce you husband and wife, you may kiss the bride."

There was a great cheer (including some zombie cheers), while

Andromedo kissed Kelly as if none of them were there except these two, and Harley started crying.

"This is the most romantic wedding I've ever been at," she cried. "I think the zombies really did it. I always wanted to be at a wedding with zombies."

"I never wanted that until now," said Tabitha. "It was a lot more romantic than I ever considered zombies at a wedding could be."

There was a great round of music for the end of the wedding ceremony, and Andromedo and Kelly ran off together. ARBOR snapped his fingers and they found themselves back at their hotel suite with all of the wedding guests with them. There was a large buffet full of exotic foods being manned as though by direct and immediate creations of ARBOR, and the room had many more chairs than the day before.

Frankfurt found Tabitha. "This has to be the most surreal day of my life, which is really saying something."

"Yeah, man, I had no idea ARBOR was such a boss at magic," said Tabitha. "I mean, I knew he was good at it, but this is over-the-top."

The president was nearby them and said enthusiastically, "This is the best wedding I've ever been to! I never thought I'd live to see a miracle of ARBOR!" He approached Frankfurt and said, "Can we be friends? I feel like everybody needs normal friends, and you two are so normal."

"I suppose after a wedding like that, the whole congregation's friends now," said Frankfurt. "Yes, we can be friends."

Tabitha laughed at the idea of them being normal. Oh how she lived a double life, one which was normal and the other that was in her opinion totally weird. Being friends with a president was weird. Tabitha then sighed and sought out Eda, considering that they were going to be friends, now, she figured her best choice in friend was the wife.

ARBOR was getting all the business today when it came to catering. The president was paying for it. He'd have done it for free, but the president insisted.

"I'm going to be going on a spacecapade soon, and I want you to come with me," George said to Frankfurt.

"Wow, that's not what you'd call terra firma, is it?" said Frankfurt, thinking about it. "I don't care, yeah, we're going! But we have to take our kids, too."

"That's fine, space is a great place for kids. It's like a cruise ship but in space."

"That sounds amazing. I would definitely like to do that."

Kelly and Andromedo disappeared into the bedroom section of the suite and locked the door.

"Well," Andromedo said to Kelly. "We're married now."

"That we are, husband."

Kelly threw herself at Andromedo and he kissed her and a bunch of stuff happened that I can't write about without possibly harming my relationship with Amazon. It was epic.

At the end of the day, Tabitha was so tired that she flew the kids to Gary's house, because it was in between both places, and asked that they stay there for the night.

"Sure, Tabitha, I love having them over," said Gary, the epitome of grandfatherly. "Speaking of, I found the money you gave me to give to the landlord, and I went and paid him for you, earlier today."

"Oh, wow, I'm much richer today than I thought," said Tabitha.

Frankfurt said, "Baby, can you fly me home? I'm so tired."

"Okay, but don't fall asleep, and you have to keep me awake.

Flying while tired is no joke."

"Okay."

And they flew back home like that, half awake and desperately trying to keep each other awake.

"You know, I'm non-religious," said Tabitha, "Yet I've been to a true miracle of ARBOR's. To me he's just a dude."

"Right, I've known that guy, like, what, 20 years," said Frankfurt. "And in all these twenty years, he's never done anything like that, until he did."

"That was amazing. I bet our grandchildren don't even believe us when we tell them this story."

"Don't get ahead of yourself. None of our kids have had kids yet, because they're all too logistically young to be having kids. Let them get established first."

"Of course." Tabitha felt her eyes starting to close and she jumped back awake and corrected course, causing a start from Frankfurt.

"Oh, baby, you have to be careful. The ground is unforgiving."

They arrived at their house barely awake, dragged themselves inside, to the bed, and were asleep mid-collapse into the bed. There they slept together for the next fourteen hours, occasionally waking up to work on having another baby. They otherwise slept like the dead.

Chapter 22

The zombies had all gotten some particularly good brains, and were amidst deep philosophical discussion by the time ARBOR had left. For one, what were they supposed to do with their time now that they were dead? Did they have to beg ARBOR to put them out of their misery? Or continue on as productive members of society?

Zombies on their part of the Earth were a pretty rare occurrence anyway, and what did one really care if your gas station attendant was a zombie? Not much, right? As long as they can do the job, and some of those zombies really do know how to manage a gas station.

Some zombies became life insurance agents. Who better to sell you on the idea that you need money after you die (for your family, you know) than someone who was dead and still having expenses? Zombies made some of the best life insurance agents.

Some of the zombies became professional wedding crashers, given that people really were going through a thing where they wanted zombies at their weddings.

Harley was talking to Sven, who attended the wedding after having been drunkenly invited.

"You're so skinny. How did you get to be so skinny?"

"I was in a mamp."

"That's a math camp, right?"

"Yes."

"Ooh, I'm sorry to hear that. I never did get what the beef was with mathematicians, anyway."

"They're jealous of our good fortune of having decent minds," said Sven with a minimal amount of bitterness.

"It's Gargantuan hospitality, but I have to fatten you up."

"What? Ha ha ha, what is this Gargantuan hospitality?"

"You should come to my house like once a week and I'll cook you something delicious."

"As long as you aren't cooking me into something delicious, ha ha ha."

"I won't eat you. I gave up eating humans years ago."

There was a pause in the conversation, and she said, "I'm joking!"

"Cannibalism is no joke. It is only sadness." A beat. "I'm joking! Cannibalism is a funny topic."

The two were laughing together an awful lot, as if they were long-time friends as opposed to strangers who'd just met twice.

"I would love to go to your home with you," said Sven, looking deep within Harley's eyes, and the two of them kissed each other merrily maybe because they were at a wedding reception and what a romantic place to be (especially considering the zombies!)

Unexpectedly, Andromedo called Frankfurt first thing in the morning. "Dude, aren't you supposed to be on your honeymoon or something?"

"That's exactly what I called you about. The president George

Franklington of the Magestic Baboon Butt wants to take us to space with him, with you guys! We're going to honeymoon in space! Whooo!"

"Right, I remember him talking about that before we left," said Frankfurt. "I guess he wants to be friends with y'all too. Friendly guy. I don't know how to act around rich and famous people."

"We'll just act like they're anybody else," plotted Andromedo. "I don't know if you heard me, but I feel like you should be excited like I am."

"I'm a little bit afraid of space-wrecks," admitted Frankfurt. "And I just woke up. It's been an eventful couple of days."

"Yeah it has been. So are you going on the spacecapade too?"

"Of course, I'll never get another opportunity like that again."

"Right, let's just hope this one doesn't crash."

"Don't talk me out of it."

Kelly called up Tabitha, who had waited until exactly then to wake up, and she said, "Did you hear that we're all going to space?"

"Yes, we're taking the kids, too."

"Oh, I hope this is an uneventful trip."

"Right, I've been having too many adventures lately and would like a nice, uneventful trip where we just see nice things and go swimming in neat places."

"Pretty lady, I don't even have a swim suit."

"But you live under-water!"

"Yes, but I guess I just forgot to buy one."

"I don't have a swim suit, either."

"Do you want to go swim suit shopping with me?"

"I would love to go swim suit shopping with you."

The two made plans to go swim suit shopping together later that day, since they were leaving to go on the spacecapade tomorrow. They met up at the Sinblossom, which was a supermarket with both groceries and goods for sale. Kelly flew there on her new broom that she'd gotten from Andromedo on their wedding day.

"Wow, I like your new broom!" Tabitha said. The old one was looking worse for wear; it was about time she got a new one. Not that she said that.

"Yeah, it was time to make an upgrade," said Kelly, and the two of them walked inside of the Sinblossom, in the goods for sale section of the supermarket.

Chapter 23

Sergeant Glen had another boss who was a joyously malevolent man who made a great comedian. His eyes were ocean blue, and his smile had canines that might and even correctly have you thinking he was a vampire. (Not that he'd admit to any such thing.) His name was David O'Malley, and he was a count from Irrorria. He had a reality TV empire where his operatives were generally shitty human beings to nice people until those nice people wanted to fight. Sergeant Glen was one of his operatives, as well as Quinn, and he followed around Sven without paying for it because Sven didn't play along like the rest of them.

David O'Malley was a true comedian, often poking fun at those around him for laughs. He really enjoyed seeing Sergeant Glen's struggles, because the bad karma of other people was funny when it wasn't his.

"You wanted to see me, sir?" said Sergeant Glen, standing with military posture, at ease.

"I just wanted to say, you're doing great work," said David O'Malley. "I really love your relationship with Tabitha. Let's see if you can develop that."

"She doesn't even like me," said Glen. "I can't develop

something that's not there."

"I really enjoyed how you antagonized her husband, but his counter antagonizing was also fun to watch."

There was a whole town and then some, being part of a reality TV show and not even knowing about it.

"You mean you laughed when he punched me?"

"It was classic! Oh, I laughed so much at that." A beat. "I think you could end up being a second husband to Tabitha if you just keep at it."

"You give terrible advice," Glen commented. "I've been particularly unlucky recently and now have to try to balance my karma, and stealing a woman who doesn't like me from her husband, whom she loves, would be terrible for my karma. I might die."

"I can pay you more if that helps," said David astutely.

"That does help." Then, "Why do you like seeing me try to break this woman up with her husband?"

"I don't know, seeing you break your heart every time is something special to me," said David. "That and seeing you get outsmarted and seeing you think you're on top of the situation only to knock you off of it. It's classic."

"I hate it when you say something's classic."

"It's not like your comfort level really is the important thing here," said David, droning on about what the viewers liked seeing and didn't like seeing. "Moreover, it's your lack of comfort that really drives viewership. I don't know why they enjoy seeing you struggle so much, but I share in the sentiment."

"I quit," he said, and David said, "Are you sure? We're going to send you on a spacecapade."

"How am I going on a spacecapade if I've quit?" he asked.

"Why would you quit if you knew you were going on a spacecapade?" asked David.

Glen thought about it.

Chapter 24

"Hello there!"

"Hello! Did I see that you got married on TruthTab? And you didn't even invite us?"

TruthTab was their internet social network. It spanned several continent and everybody in the world except for Tabitha's adoptive parents had it.

"I was so beside myself the whole time I forgot," said Kelly, to her old-time friends, Jasmine and Esmerelda. "You all know Tabitha, right?"

"Hi Tabitha," said Jasmine. "I didn't know you two were friends."

"Why, because I'm a dolphin chimera and she's a 100% human?"

"I'm distantly part-dog chimera," Tabitha said, which was only a lie because that relation was from her adoptive parents. "My people are very loyal."

"I saw her in your wedding pictures." Esmerelda said with some deep suspicion.

"That's because she's my best friend."

"You're best friends with a 100% human? How did that happen?"

"We're very much alike, have similar professional goals,

similar morals and ethics, our husbands are best friends, I could go on for a while."

"Ugh, you're married now, I'm so jealous!"

"I thought you said that you never wanted to get married, and that only suckers got married."

"Maybe I did and maybe I didn't."

"I thought that you said that only people who want to be miserable for the rest of their lives, get married."

"I don't remember saying that."

"I thought you said that only people who like eating the same food every day get married."

"Now, I definitely did not say that."

Sergeant Glen had some soul searching to do. Did he want to continue being a bad guy, or should he start on a path of being a good guy, and lose his sweet, sweet reality TV pension? He was a little bit tired of the direction of the TV show. It seemed to be him as the main character and the villain. He got one moment of heroism, and then a bunch of bad stuff happened to him, and nobody intervened to help him except for his brother Sven.

Sven was doing excellently, by the way. He was going on the spacecapade with Harley, as the two weren't very serious yet but thought it would be fun to take a trip together.

"That's a little serious, don't you think?" Glen asked Sven, when he told him about it.

"Oh, it's just some fun between friends," Sven said. "I like Harley. She's nice and she's pretty and she knows how to fly. That's an amazing combination."

"Yeah, I suppose it's alright," said Glen, annoyed that some-body liked Sven but he had nobody.

"Your time will come," said Sven, noticing the look on his

brother's face.

"My time for what?"

"Your time for romance. Your problem is you pick the wrong women."

"Who are the wrong women?"

"You know, the happily married variety that don't have any time or patience for you."

"How do you know about that?"

"Out of the horse's mouth. Word gets around."

"So you've been gossiping about me."

"No, I've been listening to gossip about you. I personally didn't believe it until just now, but here it is. You've been trying to get with a married woman and she's not interested in you. I would have thought you'd be too smart for that."

"It appears we don't know each other as well as maybe we thought."

"So are you going on the spacecapade, too?"

"Yeah, maybe."

"And not just because a certain married woman who doesn't like or appreciate you, is going too?"

"I think I'm growing on her."

"I've got a lot more money than I thought I'd get, and was wondering if you two would like to go to outer space with us," Tabitha asked Molly and Benny.

"Wow, outer space," said Benny. "We'd have to think about-"

"I'd really like to go," said Molly, interrupting him.

"That's a big gift," said Benny.

"We're family and I'd like to get to know you two," said Tabitha. "Besides, then there are more people to babysit the kids, than just the kids."

"Aha, so now we get down to the crux of the matter," said Molly jollily.

"Yes, I would like to get some romantic time in outer space with Frankfurt."

"I am just not sure about this outer space part of it," said Benny. "What if the ship blows up?"

"You two will be famous," said Tabitha. "The two who survived a math camp only to die on a spacecapade. It would make very exciting reading."

"You're joking."

"I'm half-way joking. Half-serious, you really would be famous if there was an accident. In such cases, they always take the most extraordinary people and make the story about them."

"You think we're extraordinary."

"Yes, absolutely."

"We're absolutely going," said Molly. Then she said to Benny, "Unless you absolutely don't want to go, in which case, I can stay behind."

"Oh, now that you've put it like that, it's like I have to go," said Benny. "Okay, we're going."

"Yay!" cheered Molly, with some bounce to her step.

Chapter 25

Synergy Awaits was the name of their space-cruise-liner, that everybody had signed up to go onto. This was the maiden voyage, and there was a crowd of three thousand waiting to board. Notably among them was the Irrorrian president George and his wife Eda, as he said he needed a vacation from attempted assassinations. His butler Edington was there, as they'd made their peace and he needed a butler in order to feel right. Tabitha and Frankfurt were there with all of their kids, as well as Benny and Molly. Lil' Wilbert had some stylish new clothes magicked from his old clothes, and he was feeling extra special on that day. The rest of the kids also got magical upgrades to their clothes. That was one of the advantages of having a witch as a mom, is that sometimes she was able to magic your clothes nicer.

The SA was shaped like a cruise ship for smooth design and to travel through space without the sort of problems that come with a roughly designed ship. Tabitha was looking around when she saw Harley and Sven, walking hand-in-hand and laughing about some inside joke it seemed. She was wearing Tobey and Penelope in her kangaroo-style pouch, and her back kind of hurt. The kids were seeming quite happy for this chance to go do something new and exciting, and it didn't get any newer and more exciting than going on a spacecapade.

Finally, it was boarding time. Everyone got into a very neat if convoluted line of sorts (maze of sorts nearly), and finally the family was on the ship, after some trip through the ticket masters' and then customs. The air smelled like pina coladas and salty pool water, and the crisp smell of space.

"I've never been to out space before," said Wilbert excitedly.

"A year ago today I was literally dying," said Molly with a look of grave happiness.

"A year ago today we were both literally dying, together," reminded Benny. "Too bad we have no drinks, or we could toast to being alive."

Just then a server showed up with a tray full of strawberry daiquiris and said, "Would sir and madam like daquiris for toasting?"

Benny and Molly thought about it.

"This is an all-inclusive resort, so free alcohol is everywhere," explained the server, who's nametag said he was Dave. "This is part of that free alcohol."

"Free alcohol? What?" Benny and Molly each got a strawberry daquiri and toasted each other for still being alive. Wilbert, Tom, and Jon all reached for daquiris and were sternly lectured by the server about the space ship's policy on underage drinking. Then they were taken to the Teenager Junction, where teenagers got to all hang out with each other on vacation.

"Ma'am?" approached a ship worker dressed in a fancy uniform. Tabitha started and turned to look at him, and he said, "We have a nursery for small children where they have a great time and learn about the ABCs and space from outer space."

Tabitha thought about it for a moment and told Frankfurt

that she would be back because she was going to take the kids to the nursery. She and the worker arrived at the fanciest nursery Tabitha had ever seen, resplendent with slides and monkey bars and padded everything, as well as a bouncy castle. Tobey and Penelope rushed out of their mother's kangaroo-style pouch outfit, and quickly became a part of all the action, sliding down slides, jumping in the bouncy house, etc. When it became apparent that they wouldn't miss her, she went to rejoin Frankfurt.

The ship took off like a ship in water, except it raised vertically, as if the imaginary water underneath them was rising like a tide. Within 15 minutes it was in space, and they could go to the deck to look out at outerspace.

Frankfurt and Tabitha were on the edge of the deck, kissing as if there weren't people milling around everywhere, because this was the most romantic locale they had ever visited. A minute into that, they heard a disapproving, "Ahem."

The Ahem belonged to Tabitha's biological father, the former king Henry, who was known for going on spacecapades.

"Fancy seeing you two here," he said, his good friend Thomas appearing next to him. "You're a little old to be kissing like that in public, aren't you?"

Tabitha sputtered at her father's hypocrisy. "Dad, I can't even. I've been married to this guy for close to twenty years now. I'll kiss him if I want to."

"I didn't expect to see you here," said Frankfurt to his father-in-law Henry and his good friend Thomas. They passed through a nebulae, turning the space around them magenta.

"Oh, it's good to see you!" said Thomas, grasping Frankfurt's hand with both of his hands and shaking jovially. He held on longer than expected and Frankfurt took his hand back, laughing and blushing. Frankfurt was once jealous of Thomas for hugging Tabitha when he was only wearing a tiny bathing suit, though he expected perhaps Tabitha had more reason to be jealous. "You still have that magnificent tail fin, I see."

"Yeah, I wouldn't be able to surgically get rid of it unless I didn't value my ability to walk," said Frankfurt, who had checked into it.

"I saw another guy here who had a tail fin and looked kind of like you," said Thomas to Frankfurt. "I thought he was you except he didn't recognize me and he was more svelte."

"That's my brother," said Frankfurt. "We look a lot alike."

"Hey there, you two!" chimed a cheerful voice from a few feet away. It was Sergeant Marybeth. Seemed to Tabitha like everybody had decided to go on a spacecapade at the same time. Tabitha smiled and waved at her, as if a few days ago she hadn't threatened to arrest her. (Besides, Tabitha thought, that had to be something that came up from time to time when you were good friends with a police officer, right?)

"Hi there!" Tabitha chimed back at her, and the two women hugged.

"You're not still mad at me?" Marybeth asked.

"Mad about what?" Tabitha answered with a laugh. "You should know I can't stay mad at you long. Just don't threaten to arrest me again."

"It's just it really looked for a moment there like you had kidnapped a guy."

"You should know that I would never stoop to kidnapping. I just can't think of any scenario where I would need to do such a thing."

"You never know."

"Life has been too good for me to even consider kidnapping

another person or chimera." A beat. "So how did you end up here on this spacecapade?"

"Oh, well, I had vacation time coming up, and I'd never been in space before, not since I was a little girl, so I thought, 'Why not go by myself on vacation and find myself there?'"

"If you wanted to find yourself, why not look in the mirror?" asked Tabitha in what she hoped was a helpful tone.

"Much more fun to find yourself on vacation," said Marybeth.

"Makes sense."

"Hello there!" This was Kelly. She was on the arm of one Andromedo Mr. Kelly who was smiling dopily.

"Ha, it was so crowded in here I didn't know if I'd ever find you," said Tabitha happily. The two women hugged, and then Kelly hugged Marybeth because she liked hugging people and wanted her to know that what happened at her bachelorette party, stayed there. (Marybeth, very drunk, had kissed Frankfurt, for some reason other than actually liking him, but still... It was best forgotten.) Then Andromedo hugged everybody.

Andromedo was looking happier than anybody had ever seen him. He was literally over the moon because his ladylove was now his wife. Soon Harley joined the crowd, and Andromedo appeared to be amicably jealous (an oxymoron if there ever was one) because Sven had been an exotic dancer at Kelly's bachelorette party.

"Congratulations!" Sven said, and Kelly blushed and Andromedo said, "Thank you!" with utmost sincerity. Then, "So how's the exotic dancing business going?"

"Oh, well, it is that or police officer and I do not think I would be happy as a police officer," said Sven.

Tabitha thought about how sad it was that men couldn't fly

brooms. If only men could fly brooms, like women could, Sven could get a job as a broomstick ride sharer.

"Well, if you ever want to..."

"Oh, no, this is my career and I love it."

Harley blushed. She was on a spacecapade with an exotic dancer, a very handsome one. It was at that time to Glen arrived into the group. There were several boos from the crowd.

"I am totally immune to that kind of thing," said Glen. "I'm basically part of this friend group now. Tell me, which excursion are we going to take first?"

Frankfurt said, "You are the boldest mother, I can't even call you a motherrespecter because I don't feel you give mothers proper respect." Motherrespecter was the local colloquialism. It meant serious business.

"Why can't we be friends?" asked Glen, putting an arm over Frankfurt's shoulder.

"So many reasons why we cannot be friends!" said Frankfurt.

"I'll forgive your brother and sister-in-law for trying to kill me, as well as you and Marybeth."

"Ooh, you drive a hard bargain."

"At every heart, is just another person who wants to fit in and belong."

"Why do I think that you're plotting something with this?"

"Why would I be? Do I strike you as a plotter?"

"Bruh, are you into creative writing? Because you just threw in a creative writing term."

"Did I now? Well, I do like to do a little bit of creative writing from time to time. Just to get some steam off. My mother says I'm really good."

"You have a mother?"

"Don't you?"

"No, my mom's in ARBOR'S Haven."

It was at that point that Frankfurt felt he'd said too much. The less this guy knew about him, the better.

"I'm sorry to hear that, what happened?"

"My mother had breast cancer."

"My mother is old and doesn't like many things, but she does like my writing."

"That's really nice, man. You know, you're not too bad when you're not going around playing bad cop." A beat. "Why do you go around being a bad cop?"

"Every department needs one, to use as a patsy when people complain about the police at large."

It was a dubious statement at best.

"So we're friends, now?" said Glen to Frankfurt.

"I don't know if I'd call us that. Polite enemies? Rude enemies, really. You are a rude enemy of mine."

"I have been nothing but honest with you."

"Your take on honesty. I'll admit you had been fooled, but shame on you letting yourself get fooled that way."

"A beautiful woman was throwing herself at me and I should feel ashamed of that."

"I think it's pretty brilliant that she could knock you out by pinching you."

"She is a talented woman."

"I don't know why but I feel a consistent need to punch you. Like you've given a compliment and all I can think is about punching you. It's inexplicable."

"I'm in love with your wife." He knew the fans of his semi-secret show would love that. Frankfurt punched him and he knew that the fans would love that, too. "I don't see why you're always so violent to me. I'm never violent to you. I could have you in a cell underground interrogating you until you break, but I've not done that to you. Yet."

"This is why we're not friends," said Frankfurt. "Tabitha does not love you so you're in love at my wife, not with her. She only loves me."

"Her words say one thing but her mouth says something else."

"What does her mouth say?"

Glen pantomimed kissing and Frankfurt punched him in the mouth. Blood spewed from his mouth. The two of them fought and Tabitha broke it up by kicking Glen in the shin and pushing him away from Frankfurt.

"Could the two of you not do that?" she asked.

"Why can't you love me like I love you?" asked Glen plaintively.

"I'm married!"

"You don't kiss like you're married."

"Have we ever kissed when I wasn't under duress?"

"That's besides the point."

"No it's not. If we'd ever kissed while I wasn't under duress, maybe you could take it seriously. But since we only ever kissed while I was under duress, maybe you should reevaluate your life."

"How should I reevaluate my life?"

"I think you should think about that, while Frankfurt and I go to enjoy our vacation," she said, grabbing Frankfurt by the hand and taking him away from Glen. She and Frankfurt walked from the promenade into a bar.

"How could you kiss a guy like that?" asked Frankfurt.

"It was so I could pinch the back of his neck to knock him out. One could say I'm alive today because I kissed that toad."

"What a toad of a man he is! Does he have any redeeming

qualities?"

"He can be nice from time to time."

They sat down at the bar, and Tabitha ordered a pina colada while Frankfurt ordered an Irrorrian whiskey. The bartender was a dolphin chimera who looked more dolphin than human but stood on two legs and had opposable thumbs. His name tag said Billy, and he was wearing a fancy red uniform.

"Marital problems?" he asked, in full bartender mode.

"What, no, never," said Tabitha, forgetting that just a few days ago, they were on a break.

"Do you have a wife?" Frankfurt asked Billy.

"Oh, no, this lifestyle is not conducive to being married," said Billy. "I work 12 hours a day every day, no days off. But I do have a crush." He smiled wickedly.

"Don't get married," said Frankfurt. Tabitha gasped. "These women just break your heart again and again and you go back for more because you can't imagine life without them."

"That sounds horrible," said Billy.

"It is," said Frankfurt.

"Are you saying that you regret getting married to me?" asked Tabitha, hurt.

"No."

"Then what are you saying?"

"That you break my heart again and again and we're still together because I can't imagine life without you."

"I really don't mean to break your heart."

"How did you break his heart?" asked the very nosy Billy.

"None of your beeswax," said Tabitha, and Billy gave her a look like her next drink might be suspect.

"She kissed another guy."

"I was under duress!" she said for what felt like the millionth time.

"Gurl, how can you kiss a man under duress?" asked Billy, putting a hand on his hip.

"Seriously," said Tabitha to Frankfurt. "I don't want to tell this dolphin my whole life story."

Frankfurt, because he couldn't help himself, kissed her briefly and then said, "I don't mind. We're in space. I could get really into telling your whole life story."

"Ugh!" said Tabitha, and walked off, abandoning Frankfurt to the bar, in hopes of finding Harley and Kelly, and maybe Marybeth.

Soon after she walked out of the bar, Marybeth walked into it. She saw Frankfurt and sat down next to him. He was not happy.

"You police are the worst!" he said unfairly.

"Don't lump me in with Glen."

"Yeah, the both of you have kissed my wife."

"I kissed you, too, though."

"Yeah, why did you do that? You got me into so much trouble."

"I thought it would even the score between you and Tabitha, since she kissed another person, for you to have kissed another person."

"Oh, so you want to help me make Tabitha jealous, then, hm?"

"No offense, but I'd rather help Tabitha make you jealous, then to help you make Tabitha jealous."

"Why? Is she just the more attractive spouse? I always knew it!"

"Because she's my friend and I don't have that many friends. Whereas you're just her jealous husband who called me a harlot."

"I'm sorry about that," he said.

Billy turned his attention to Marybeth and said, "And what

would you like to drink, young lady?"

"Ugh, soda," she said, having spent too much of the book series drunk.

"One soda coming right up." He winked at Frankfurt, who felt very uncomfortable at that, seeing as how he didn't need any more trouble with his wife.

Meanwhile, Tabitha was looking for Kelly, but Harley found her first.

"You want to go on an excursion with me?" Harley asked. She was holding a space suit.

Tabitha thought about it for a moment and then said, "Sure!" A beat. "What are we doing?"

"We're going into space to swim in the nebula," said Harley. "Come on, let's get you a suit."

Soon afterwards, Harley and Tabitha were in space suits, boarding a smaller space ship to go nebula swimming. The nebula, which they called the Sea Horse Nebula, was very bright around them, casting a magenta glow on their space suits.

"Ooh, I can't wait to do this," said Harley.

"Where's Sven?" Tabitha asked.

"Oh, he found a lady's club and asked about a job and I haven't seen him since," said Harley with a touch of sadness in her voice. "It doesn't matter. That's his career and I support him."

"Are you two an item now?" asked Tabitha.

"No, but maybe moving in that direction. I don't know if I can handle the jealousy of being with an exotic dancer, you know."

Tabitha took a moment to imagine Frankfurt as an exotic dancer, and the idea kind of tickled her fancy. With a dolphin tail like he had on his lower back, he'd make all the money, surely. It was probably good that he wasn't an exotic dancer. The two of them wouldn't know what to do with so much money.

It was time to go out into space, so Harley and Tabitha got into line to go out into the nebula, and there was a pusher at the beginning of the line, pushing all of the timid excursion goers out into space, to get over their initial hesitation.

"Wait," said Tabitha, and the pusher pushed her out into the nebula.

Tabitha had never seen anything so beautiful before in her life, except maybe her kids. There was no horizon, just bright magenta clouds of hydrogen everywhere. She looked over at Harley, who's facial expression changed from scared to enthralled in seconds.

"Don't you wish you could fly a broom through this?" she asked Harley, but Harley couldn't hear her. No matter. The two of them went swimming, pretending that they were synchronized swimmers.

Chapter 26

There was a commotion back in the promenade, on the main ship. A couple of humans were in an argument and one beat the other over the head with a lunch tray. Frankfurt and Marybeth went to investigate, being nosy, but it was quickly handled by the ship's security.

"Would you like to go on an excursion with me?" Marybeth asked him.

"No, the last thing I need in my life is for Tabitha to think I'm spending too much time with another woman," said Frankfurt.

"I don't think she'll think that," said Marybeth. "Besides, she already punched me, and I don't want to get punched by her again, so there's no chance of me putting the moves on you."

"Too late, that ship's already sailed," said Frankfurt, and went back into the bar to get drunker. Marybeth followed him, and ordered a margarita.

"Why are you still here?" asked Frankfurt.

"I don't know anybody else on the ship who's nearby," said Marybeth. She briefly remembered kissing him and blushed. Frankfurt was a handsome guy, but he was Tabitha's handsome guy.

Billy handed Marybeth her margarita and Frankfurt more

Irrorrian whiskey, and said, "So, here's your chance to make your wife jealous."

"Billy, you are a bad bartender," said Frankfurt. "What in all of outer space makes you think I want to make my wife jealous? She. Is. A. Witch. She could curse me to the next generation."

"She made you jealous," said Billy coyly. Then, "You know, I get off of this shift in just a few minutes. Maybe I could help you make her jealous."

Frankfurt sputtered. "I'm flattered, but no thank you."

"Aren't you Mr. Popular?" asked Marybeth with a touch of bitter sarcasm in her voice. She took a deep drink of her margarita.

A few drinks in, Frankfurt and Marybeth were suddenly good friends, and they went together to go sing, "My Majestic Baboon Butt," which was the rap song commissioned by George Franklington, the president of Irrorria. The problem was, neither of them really knew the words to the song, which was a common problem because the rapper was a notorious mumbler.

"What What
There's nothing but
Glory for my majestic baboon butt
You know what
The ladies always want
My majestic baboon butt
Tell you what..."

And it went on that way, wrongly, for the whole song. They did absolutely terribly at it, and the crowd, loving bad karaoke, went wild for it. The two, high on a good karaoke session, went back to their seats to go drink some more.

"We were really good at that," said Marybeth.

"Yeah, we were," said Frankfurt, fonder of Marybeth than he'd ever been. He had to admit having some small amount of prejudice towards her ever since that time she kissed Tabitha, but alcohol and karaoke were curing him of that. "Maybe we should part ways. You're never going to find a man sitting next to me."

"What makes you think I want to find a man?" asked Marybeth.

Frankfurt thought about that. "I thought that's what single people did on vacation, find someone to cohort with, you know? And I am not that person."

"That is too bad," said Billy the bartender, who had left the other side of the bar to go drinking on that side of the bar. "You are too handsome to be married to a woman who doesn't appreciate you."

"What makes you think my wife doesn't appreciate me?" asked Frankfurt, kind of annoyed.

"She kissed another man," said Billy.

"This harlot next to me kissed me," said Frankfurt, taking up for Tabitha in a way she wouldn't approve of.

"Hey!" said Marybeth. "I really thought I was doing you a favor."

"Don't do me any favors," said Frankfurt.

Tabitha and Harley came back from their nebula excursion high on outer space and very happy with each other.

"Do you want to get a drink with me?" asked Harley.

"Sure!" said Tabitha, who wasn't due to pick up her kids for several hours. They walked back into the bar where Frankfurt and Marybeth were sitting.

"And here comes the unappreciative wife!" said Billy cattily.

"Billy, you must not care about your job," said Tabitha crossly. "I very much appreciate my husband."

"Then why did you kiss another man?"

"I knocked out the guy shortly after kissing him so that I could steal his clothes and escape from prison."

"Ooh, now this is getting juicy," said Billy. "And what were you in prison for?"

"None of your beeswax, that's what."

She was in prison for being a royal. She'd have stayed longer, but being magic helped remedy the situation.

"Are you a criminal?" Billy asked conspiratorially.

"No. It was a case of mistaken identity."

Billy sighed. "It seems like everybody here has a more interesting life than I do." As if that was a good thing for them.

"You work on a space ship," said Tabitha. "That's like if I complained that my job isn't interesting."

"Ooh, and what do you do?" asked Billy.

"I'm a broomstick ride sharer."

"Oh, that does sound interesting," he said.

"It's alright. It's a job."

"Gurl, make that money."

"Now, am I being completely crazy here, or were you hitting on my husband?" asked Tabitha mildly.

"You're being completely crazy," said Billy, but Frankfurt said, "Yes, he was hitting on me."

"Don't be an opportunistic cunt," said Tabitha. Billy was taken aback by her choice of words, but he'd had worse reactions to his flirtations in the past.

"I don't know how to respond to that," he said.

"You don't have to respond," said Tabitha. "Just think about it, let it sink in..."

The ship had some turbulence, and everybody started.

"What was that?" George asked Edington, whom he'd forgiven without much groveling at all from Edington. Edington was not normally the type to grovel, but he was so embarrassed for having to tried to kill his boss/best friend. He wasn't back to his old self, yet. He was decidedly depressed at the idea that there were mind control drugs out there and that he and his boss had fallen victim to them.

"I don't know," said Edington morosely. "Seems like nothing works like it's supposed to anymore."

"I need you to snap out of it," said George with gentle humor, more than he'd normally afford for his butler. "Get back to your usual sarcastic self. I can't handle your depression."

"Depression is a chemical problem," said Edington. "I'm environmentally sad."

"I don't think you know as much about it as you think you do," said Eda, who was also very fond of Edington, to the point of mild jealousy because she felt as if George loved Edington more than he loved her. "Either way, buck up, lil' man."

The lights flickered on and off, then on again.

"This is supposed to be the nicest space cruise ship there is," said George. "I wonder what all the trouble is."

"The world is falling apart around us," Edington moaned. "Next thing you know, there will be a murder and all of us will be suspects."

"That's silly," said George. "For the most part, none of us have ever tried to kill anybody."

"Yeah, except when I tried to kill you a few days ago."

"Get over it already. You had no control over it. And you're lucky. There are very few heads of state who would react so kindly to this, but you're my best friend, so there's that." A beat. "Would you still be my best friend if I wasn't a super-rich head of state?"

"I think I'd like you better if you weren't a super-rich head of state," said Edington with his usual brutal honesty.

"Thank you, I needed to hear that."

They went out of their suite to go investigate. The lights flickered again, and people were beginning to panic. What if this meant that the ship was about to lose power, in space? There were many places that it was okay to lose power, but space wasn't one of them.

Edington caught a glimpse of space out of the corner of his eye. They were leaving the nebula, but still in the thick of it, and the outside was a bright pink.

Chapter 27

Harley said, "I don't think this is supposed to happen," at all the flickering on and off of the lights. "I hope the ship isn't breaking down." She was a responsible drinker, most of the time, and had only had a little bit too much of her pirate's rum. Harley was pirate stock, not that you could tell unless you were looking for it, but she looked as if she could be ransacking a ship and stealing all the booty. She must have been some other stock, too, though, because she had a spirit as gentle and kind as a butterfly.

"This is the nicest space ship there is," said Tabitha. "If it breaks down, that would be phenomenally bad."

"Say that again?"

"Say what again?"

"Phenomenally."

"Phenomenally."

"Hahaha, that's a funny word. It's crazy we know how to pronounce it."

"Ha, you're drunk," Tabitha said drunkenly to Harley. Then, "We should go check on the kids."

Frankfurt said, "Do you want me to go with you?"

"I can go with you," Harley volunteered.

"You stay here and fend off your wannabe lovers," Tabitha said with a laugh. "I'll go with Harley."

Frankfurt scowled, and Harley and Tabitha left the bar.

They first went to check on the babies, since the older kids were 1) further away and 2) presumably could take care of themselves. Tobey and Penelope were in a bouncy house, bouncing, and when Tabitha tried to pick them up, they screamed because they wanted to keep bouncing.

"It's not time for them to go yet," said a bossy little woman who was about a head shorter than Tabitha and half a head shorter than Harley. Her nametag said Meg. "It's best if parents pick up their children all at the same time."

"I was just checking on them," said Tabitha to Meg, who gave her a disapproving look.

"Okay, well, please in the future, keep your checking on them until it's time to pick them up," said Meg, waving a hand in front of her nose to ward off the smell of alcohol.

Tabitha thought about saying something to Meg about being rude to her on her first vacation in a decade, but Harley pulled her arm, and they instead went looking for the teenagers.

"These young people have no respect," said Tabitha, annoyed. "They feed you alcohol like they're going to harvest your liver for foie gras, and then they judge you for it."

"You're just not a great drinker," said Harley. "Because you don't drink often."

"Seems like I've been drinking more than usual, lately," grumbled Tabitha.

"That's okay. Nobody's perfect."

They came to the Teen Central and both perused the crowd for Tabitha's teenagers. Wilbert was the first one they spotted.

"Marissa!" Tabitha shouted.

Wilbert almost ignored her, then came back and said, "Mom, you're supposed to call me Wilbert."

"Ooh, sorry about that," said Tabitha, who'd expected that Wilbert would be tired of being a boy by now. He wasn't. He loved being a boy. "Wilbert, where are your brothers?"

"They're with some girls," said Wilbert conspiratorially. "I think we should leave them alone."

"Why would I leave them alone just because they're with girls?" Tabitha said. "That doesn't even make any sense. You kids nowadays have no idea how parenting works."

"How does parenting work?" asked Wilbert, amused at his mother.

"Well, if they're cohorting with the opposite sex, you're supposed to be there glaring at them," said Harley for Tabitha's sake.

"That's true," said Tabitha. "Your grandfather used to glare at me all the time. Now I'm one of his favorite people. It's a process."

Wilbert made a pfft noise. "I've never seen Grandpa glare at anybody."

"There's a lot about your grandfather that you just don't know," said Tabitha. The lights flickered on and off again. "What is that?"

"I don't know," said Wilbert, "but I'd be lying if I said it didn't make me nervous."

The Teen Central supervisor approached Tabitha much in the same way as the Baby Central supervisor did, except for more politely.

"Madam, are you here to pick up your teenagers?" he asked, barely older than a teenager himself. His name was Max; said so on his nametag. "Because normally for the sake of normalcy, we encourage parents to leave their children until it's time to pick them up."

"I was just checking on them," said Tabitha, trying to keep the annoyance out of her voice. "Seeing as how the lights keep flickering on and off."

"It's just a little bit of space turbulence," explained Max. "The nebulas can be problematic." Seeing as how the women seemed satisfied with his explanation, he guided them back to what he called Grownup Central, which was where the grownups were supposed to be. They waved goodbye to Wilbert, who shyly waved back at them.

"I don't know what to make of these strangers thinking they can tell me what to do when it comes to my kids," said Tabitha.

Harley said, "Ah, don't worry about it. They tell you that so you can relax during the trip while they take care of your kids."

"I appreciate them for it," said Tabitha, "but their attitude rubs me the wrong way."

"You're getting in the way of them doing their job," said Harley. "How would you like it if somebody who you weren't supposed to be giving a ride to, came to your broom and started asking questions?"

"I don't know, that's never happened to me," said Tabitha. "I do get backseat fliers every now and again, but that's just because they're nervous because falling would be unpleasant."

There was a scream, a high-pitched shriek, as the lights went out again, and stayed out.

"See, they can say nothing's wrong," said Tabitha, beginning to panic, "but that shrieking noise has me thinking otherwise."

"My witch's sense is activated," said Harley. "Something's wrong."

Fumbling about blindly in the dark, they quickly made their

way to the source of the scream. It took a moment for the lights to come back on, but when they did, Harley and Tabitha were astonished by what they saw. It was Sven, standing next to Glen, horror-struck and on his knees, and covered in Glen's blood. Glen was very dead on the ground, in a pool of his own blood.

To be continued...

9 798359 088046